A LION BY THE MANE

English veterinary-surgeon Margaret Ward is being flown from Cape Town to a Game Reserve in the Transvaal. The pilot is the younger partner in Schroeder Freight Ltd., but Jan Schroeder is a man struggling to prove himself and the flight ends in disaster of his own making. Margaret is smugly convinced she can tame the headstrong pilot, but when Jan leaps from one disaster to another Margaret stubbornly follows him into a vortex of danger, tribal witchcraft and tangled emotions.

EVA DANE

A LION BY THE MANE

Complete and Unabridged

ULVERSCROFT
Leicester

First published in Great Britain in 1977 by
Macdonald & Jane's Publishers Ltd.,
London

First Large Print Edition
published April 1986

British Library CIP Data

Dane, Eva
  A lion by the mane.—Large print ed.
  Ulverscroft large print series: romance
  Rn: Edna Dawes   I. Title
  823′.914[F]   PR6054.A46/

  ISBN 0-7089-1445-4

Published by
F. A. Thorpe (Publishing) Ltd.
Anstey, Leicestershire
Set by Rowland Phototypesetting Ltd.
Bury St. Edmunds, Suffolk
Printed and bound in Great Britain by
T. J. Press (Padstow) Ltd., Padstow, Cornwall

1

IT had not really been a wasted afternoon because Margaret had enjoyed the ride through Sea Point in glorious Cape sunshine, but her host had taken a less philosophical view of the non-appearance of the man she had been invited to meet. In short, Chris Schroeder had been flaming mad! His wife, Helen, had done her best to damp down the long-standing irascibility towards his youngest brother, but Chris had talked her down.

"Don't waste your time inventing reasons why he may have been detained. Jan is completely unreliable and irresponsible! No doubt he is stretched out on the beach with whoever he is taking around these days, and has not even read my message. I'll be charitable enough to assume he *hasn't* read it, although it's more than likely he has chosen to ignore anything I write to him."

At four-thirty, an hour past the time Jan Schroeder should have arrived, Margaret assured her host she was not a bit put out, that she had enjoyed chatting to Helen, and stood up to leave. The Schroeders were still not used to guests who travelled by bicycle, although Margaret had told them she was a health-addict when they first met. Now, she hid a smile at the self-conscious way they stood on the *stoep* watching her set off. The entrance to the house was too imposing for a mere bicycle; her two-wheeled machine couldn't achieve the flourishing sweep which the curving driveway deserved, but she did her best not to wobble as she gave a farewell wave.

She did not regret buying the bicycle. For such a short stay in Cape Town it was not worth hiring a car, and she was enough of a newcomer to South Africa to revel in a December summer which was better enjoyed in the open air than zipping every-where shut in with petrol fumes. Free-wheeling down the last curve of the drive she found herself envying Helen Schroeder, who had married for love and settled in this part of the world. From the little she knew of the couple, it seemed Helen had left only an elderly disinterested father in England and had never been back to the country of her birth. Could I do that? thought Margaret. Could I cut myself off from my parents and my sister to devote my life to a free-lance pilot who flies unusual cargoes across wild bush country? Maybe . . . if the man was like Chris Schroeder!

She inhaled the scent of blossoms in the garden. Under the powerful sun the perfumes were heady, drugging her senses with sleepy pleasure. A sigh of contentment escaped her as she rolled smoothly along, first in the dappled shadow of an over-hanging tree, then in brilliant sunshine. No, it had not been a wasted afternoon. The visit to these friendly people had been reward enough. It did not matter that Jan Schroeder had stayed away.

Then, a roaring, screaming, dust-clouded streak of orange hurtled through the wide gates from the road and slewed sideways, kicking up a spray of small stones as the driver stamped on the brakes. He was not quite quick enough. The front wheel of Margaret's bicycle buckled beneath the onslaught, and she spun through the air to land with a jarring thud several feet away. Vaguely, through the pain in her back, she was aware of someone

3

leaping the low bushes to reach her but her vision came and went like ripples breaking the surface of a reflection in water.

"Can you move?" she was asked.

"I think so." Her eyes remained closed to steady the giddy circling of the tree-tops above her.

Protests that there was no need to carry her seemed to fall on deaf ears, and she was still in a dazed condition several minutes later when Chris and Helen hurried on to the *stoep* with shocked exclamations at the state of their recently-departed guest. Jan Schroeder's chances of a warm welcome had been pretty thin before; now, he didn't stand a chance! Throughout the terse cross-talk between the brothers it seemed to Margaret that Jan made the most of his part in the accident, almost as if he took a vicious pleasure in living up to Chris's low opinion of him.

Once she was on the settee, the room stopped waltzing and it was possible for her to keep her eyes open.

"Feeling steadier?" asked Helen anxiously.

"Yes, I'm fine . . . really. I was simply stunned for a few minutes." She raised her head to look at the two men. "Please stop apportioning blame. There is no need."

"What were you doing on that obsolete pedal-pusher, for God's sake?" asked Jan. "I was hardly expecting a bicycle at four-thirty in a residential area like this. You're not a delivery-boy, are you?"

Margaret would have laughed. There was a kind of audacious forthrightness about this younger Schroeder which appealed to her. His lack of fuss and the "damn-all" honesty he adopted with regard to the situation didn't suit his brother one bit, however, and Chris's face hardened when he said, "Margaret . . . Miss Ward . . . is a friend of ours and I'd appreciate it if you would adopt a more conventional style of manners while you are in my home. I haven't yet heard you apologize."

Jan gave a half-bow and said, "I apologize, Miss Ward." Realization suddenly dawned across his much-freckled face. "You are the woman vet I was supposed to meet."

She smiled. "I was going to say 'you nearly missed me' but my battered bicycle gives it the lie."

"You were leaving! Why didn't you wait for me?"

"I did," she protested. "In case your watch has stopped, it is now well over an hour past the time you were supposed to arrive."

"I was hurrying—you may have noticed," he said briefly. "You don't take that pedal-machine seriously, do you? I confess you look too young and enticing to be an animal doctor, but as a professional woman you should have more dignity. The first thing I noticed as I drove in was the flash of bare legs. Your skirt was well above . . ."

"Jan!" warned Helen in a low voice, glancing at her husband, and Margaret had the impression of secret sympathy flowing from the woman to her erring brother-in-law.

"We are still waiting to hear your excuse for being late," commented Chris. "You do have one, I take it?"

"Yes, I have one," replied Jan tightly, "but surely it is more important for me to talk to Miss Ward first. She is the reason I was invited, after all."

Helen intervened as she had on many

occasions. "Yes, and as an Englishwoman myself, I know just what Margaret needs at the moment. A cup of tea." She smiled at the other girl. "Am I right?"

"How did you guess?" she replied, grateful for the way her hostess was keeping the emotional temperature down. She swung her legs off the settee and asked Chris, "Has Helen imbued you with many English ways?"

He relaxed slightly and sat down. "When a very determined woman sets her mind to something, she usually succeeds, but luckily, South Africa has charmed her so much, I have escaped very lightly."

"Are *you* a very determined woman?" asked Jan, still standing in the centre of the room.

She considered. "So far, I have not had very much reason to be. Fortune has smiled on me to a great extent, and I have never had to fight for something against all odds."

"So this job at the Game Reserve was handed to you on a plate?"

"In a way, I suppose it was," she agreed, "although it isn't a permanent appointment, you know. Doctor Eggerton simply arranged for me to spend a short time with

Russell Martin so that I could further my ecological studies. We don't have that much big game in England." She leant back against the cushions. "It was pure chance which brought me the introduction to Doctor Eggerton. I had not the slightest idea that he would be the means of achieving my ambition to study African wild life at close quarters." She gave a swift smile. "See what I mean about not having to fight against all odds?"

Helen re-entered the room. "Tea will be along shortly. Your colour has returned, Margaret. That's a good sign."

"I have been talking about the great love of my life, that's why. Good thing you interrupted me. Once I start on that subject I am liable to become boring," the girl replied gaily, but Helen had not seen such flushed cheeks and luminous green eyes when her guest had talked about animals earlier.

"For heaven's sake, sit down, Jan," she told her brother-in-law. "You look all set to dash away again at the first opportunity. I know nothing will induce you to drink tea, so get yourself a whisky—although

8

how you can stomach it at this hour, I don't know—and relax in that chair."

"You're not expecting other visitors, are you, because my car is very effectively blocking your driveway?" He walked to the sideboard and poured a sizeable drink before returning to sit beside Margaret. "I've arranged an early take-off on Wednesday. Hope that won't bother you too much," he said to her.

"Not a bit. How long will it take to fly there?"

"Five hours, or so."

"Eh?" said Chris. "How are you going —via Nairobi?"

"I'm taking a Dakota. It's a lot slower than the Trilander."

"You are taking a what!"

Jan stiffened. "A Dakota. I collected it today, that's why I am late. I only touched down at three this afternoon."

Chris had risen again and gripped the back of the leather armchair in an effort to keep calm. "Would you mind telling me quickly and calmly just how you arranged to collect a Dakota and why you are flying it up to Myala."

Jan rose, too, tossing back the drink as

he did so. "The Valetta needs a lengthy service before either of us takes it up again, and you are using the Trilander for those two trips to Kimberley. Van Heerdon told me about this . . ."

"Ah, now we are getting to the truth!" interrupted Chris savagely. "I guessed Van Heerdon featured in it somewhere. What does it take to convince you that man means trouble!"

"I went over this machine inch by inch before I bought it. I'm not a fool, Chris. Just for once, why don't you admit I know more about aircraft than you do?"

"Pity you don't know a little more about people. Van Heerdon is a crook and everyone but you can see it. I warned you last time that I have no intention of being involved in any more deals which spring from him—or anyone connected with him. That Dakota can go back on the scrap heap it came from. That's final, Jan. The company will not finance a deal in obsolete aircraft."

"The company doesn't have to," said Jan banging his glass on the table. "I'll buy it myself."

"You're crazy! That orange danger-machine you drive ruined your bank balance."

"I'll manage. Van Heerdon is prepared to take payment in instalments. It was a damned sight cheaper than any other aircraft, and it was available *now*. I wouldn't let the Valetta make another trip without stripping it right down, so would you rather I left Russell Martin without stores for another month? We have to have another machine if we are to fulfil our contracts. You agreed—the whole family agreed—that I should look out for a suitable aircraft."

"Yes, but we didn't mean a flaming useless heap of scrap-metal," stormed Chris.

Helen had had enough. "If you two are going to have a row, would you mind going into the study," she said calmly. "Margaret is trying to recover from being knocked from her bicycle, and neither of us wishes to hear the heated arguments of two business executives—especially when the whole transaction appears to be a *fait accompli*."

Chris looked at the two women and

apologized. "We got carried away. I'm sorry."

Jan crossed the room angrily. "I'll leave. Every time I come here I ruin your social routine, Helen. I'm surprised you continue to invite me."

"I haven't finished yet," snapped Chris, following his brother. "We'll thrash this matter out before you go, if you don't mind."

"You can bloody-well thrash as much as you like, it won't alter the fact that the Dakota is part of Schroeder Freight Limited as from today."

The closing door muffled any further comment and Margaret stared after the two men with confused thoughts. Physically, the brothers were similar enough. Both six-footers and hard-muscled, with Jan the slightly leaner of the two, and with red hair instead of blond. They had that outdoor healthy look which was striking rather than handsome, and it would be difficult to tell which was speaking if he were not visible. However, as far as temperament was concerned there was plainly a wide difference between them. Helen elaborated on this as she apologized for the two men.

"As soon as Jan was fifteen minutes late I knew this was liable to happen." She poured tea which had just been brought, and handed a cup to her guest. "He riles Chris in just about every way he can. You have met Chris on three occasions, and you'll agree that he is normally a very reasonable, level-headed man."

"He's a charmer," agreed Margaret. "I'm very envious."

"Yet, as soon as Jan comes on the scene, he becomes edgy, truculent, and almost a stranger. It's getting worse. Chris anticipates the discord and starts arguing mentally with Jan before he arrives."

"Yes, I noticed he had already decided that his brother was on the beach with a girl-friend when he should have been here."

"Nine times out of ten, he would have been. Today, Jan had a legitimate excuse, although I suspect it will cause more trouble than if he *had* been on the beach," she reflected.

"Why did they go into business together if they are so incompatible? It's hardly a good basis on which to run a company," said Margaret in curiosity.

"It wasn't always like this," explained Helen, leaning back with a dreamy look in her eyes. "When I married Chris he had just lost the one aircraft he owned in an uprising in East Africa, and the family joined forces to set him up in business again. Each male member bought a share in the new company, although Chris was to run it as he had before. The difference was that the shareholders divided the profits *and* the losses." She smiled faintly. "We were broke for the first five years of our marriage."

"I'd never guess it," put in Margaret. "Your home is lovely."

"Thank you. To be fair to Jan, he suffered as much as we did at the beginning. He had just finished his apprenticeship as an aircraft mechanic and kept his promise to Chris to join the company regardless of the state it was in. He worked for a small wage, but Chris gave him flying lessons in lieu. He learnt very quickly and in no time was demanding the purchase of another machine. It would have meant a big loan from the bank, so Jan was outvoted by the cautious shareholders. He took the decision as a personal distrust of his ability,

14

and things deteriorated from then on." She sighed. "I think the time is coming when Jan will break away and start up on his own. Chris and I are doing our best to prevent it, but he really is impossible, at times."

"I should have thought Chris would be glad to see him go if their relationship is one long argument."

Helen took Margaret's cup and refilled it. "Oh, they're not at each other's throats the whole time. The Schroeders have a very strong family feeling which binds them, and Chris and Jan admire certain facets of the other's character. Jan has never quite forgotten his early hero-worship of an older brother who became what he himself most wanted to be and worked like a slave to become—a pilot, too. Chris was tremendously proud of his pupil and, if he is honest, admits that Jan is the better flier. Unfortunately, it means he takes risks. Chris is a good pilot—I have personal experience of that—so he condemns the dare-devil attitude Jan adopts. Criticism is only a spur to increase his recklessness, as far as Jan is concerned, and there you have the situation. Jan is fearless and carries off his stunts with ease, but it is not the way to run a freight company. Chris is right."

"Yet you protect Jan."

Helen lifted her grey eyes to meet the green ones. "You noticed?"

"Loyal as you are to your husband, you still keep an impartial manner when they quarrel. Are you sorry for Jan?"

"No one could be sorry for Jan—he wouldn't allow them to be," she said with conviction. "Perhaps it is that I understand why he behaves as he does. It can't be easy to be the youngest of five brothers and two brothers-in-law, all of them extremely successful in their chosen fields."

"*Five* brothers! Heavens, that must take a lot of living up to." Margaret's mind baulked at the thought of five Schroeder men all as magnetic as the two she had already met.

Warmth crept into Helen's voice as she described the family she had married into. "The Schroeders are a fantastic group of people. The men are all big, strong, and fiercely male; the women are dark and pretty. There is a very strong blood tie between them and they close ranks the minute one of their number is threatened.

The brothers have built very flourishing careers, and the two girls married equally successful professional men."

"Mmm," said Margaret, beginning to see the set-up. "And Jan, as the youngest, feels bound to hold his own amongst them."

"More than that," corrected Helen, "he fights a perpetual battle to prove he can do anything they can do—and better! From what I can deduce, I think Jan had a pretty thin time of it as a boy. Being the youngest, he was always the one who had to find the others in games of hide and seek. On a large farm, four enterprising boys and two crafty girls can stay concealed all day if they wish, and Jan used to tramp for miles on his young legs trying to find them. In the war games, there was never any question of who was to be taken prisoner and tortured. Of course, they didn't really hurt him, but I think they put the fear of God into him sometimes. Boys can be very cruel to each other through thoughtlessness. I know they tied poor Jan to a tree once, then went home and forgot about him. They all had a thrashing for that. Chris said he couldn't sit down for several days, because it had been his idea in the first place. He seems to have been the ring-leader, I fear. He is the second eldest, and together with Kip, who is barely a year younger, dreamt up most of the games they all played. Even today, the two of them are as close as twins, but Kip has a farm which he refuses to give up to join in the risky business of flying. Chris has always regretted his inability to persuade him."

"Is Jan younger than the girls?"

"Yes. George, the barrister of the family, is four years older and the girls fit in between him and Kip. As Jan got older, he shot up and developed very quickly but, unfortunately for him, so did all the others. When he started dating girls, he was really put through the mill by his more experienced brothers. You can imagine the sort of thing, can't you! A long drawn-out stag party. Chris pointed out to me that they all went through it in turn, but he forgets Jan was the only one who never had the satisfaction of getting his own back on a younger one. Mind you, there was the other side of the coin. The brothers often lent him money for something he desperately wanted or covered up for him when he had been up to mischief, and if any school-fellow dared cross swords with him, the family sorted out the miscreant in no uncertain terms. Reading between the lines, I suspect the Schroeder children terrorized the whole school by sheer force of numbers. The girls were no exception. Chris says they had a deadly kick to the shins."

Margaret laughed. "A charming family all round! I see what you mean by the strong blood tie. How does the rest of the family get on with Jan now?"

"They are all beginning to lose patience, I'm sorry to say. They put his temperament down to the fact that he is the only one with red hair, but it goes much deeper than that, in my opinion. I try to put in a good word for him when I can because I can understand the motivation for his actions, but I don't agree with his unreasonable desire to go one better all the time. The fastest cars, the fastest girls, the most expensive flat—and now he is trying to prove he is more successful at the air-freight business than Chris."

"And is he?"

"No," said Helen immediately. "On the flying side he can hardly be equalled—he has never failed to deliver a cargo—but he falls down on the business side. His association with Van Heerdon has ruined that. The desire to make money fast has led him to accept assignments Chris would never consider, and that is really the biggest bone of contention between them. Every time Jan flies a doubtful cargo he puts the good name of the firm at risk."

At this point there was the sound of loud voices followed by a banging door. Margaret glanced through the long window to see Jan take the steps two at a time and stride away down the drive. She felt a pang of disappointment. Helen's words had set up a vision of a small freckle-faced boy with red-gold hair fighting to hide his fear of his brothers' blood-thirsty threats of torture, and of an adolescent youth unable to turn off their ribaldry the way a more mature man would. Sympathy welled up in her— but Jan would allow no one to feel sorry for him, Helen said. Now, he had gone without a further word, leaving her in a strange limbo; as if she had glimpsed excitement through a door which closed in her face to reveal the words NO ENTRY.

"He's gone!" She had not meant to sound so desolate.

"Oh dear, that means Chris will be angry all the evening," said Helen absently. Her guest's reaction was worrying her. The crusading light had already appeared in her eyes, and as one who had suffered in the same way nine years ago, she felt some alarm. It might almost be a repeat performance; an English girl, a South African pilot, and a flight across country ahead of them. But there were two major variations. Jan was a vastly different prospect from Chris, and their journey was not likely to lead them into the midst of an East African uprising, as hers had. If Fate was kind to Margaret, Jan would fly her to Myala, then vanish from her life. "He might have made the final arrangements before he left," she complained to cover her brief silence. "How typical of him to walk out like that."

"Perhaps he resented his actions being criticized in front of a stranger," put in Margaret thoughtfully. "If he is out to prove himself, it hardly furthered his cause."

"That's why I sent them out. I guessed the sparks would fly."

Margaret started to feel her way carefully. "Jan is lucky to have an ally in you. What about his girl-friend . . . does she try to help him?"

Helen knew what the other girl was doing and sighed inwardly. "If I tell you I never know from day to day who the present girl is you'll realize that Jan only mixes with swinging sex-symbols. All they care about is his reputation for excitement and recklessness. It would never occur to any of them to discover what is beneath that surface bravado."

"Then it's time someone did."

Helen couldn't hold out any longer. "The odds are against you, Margaret. In two days' time you'll be flying up to Myala."

"He'll be coming with me," she said calmly.

"And leaving again! You can't catch a lion by the mane. You either throw a net over him and leave him snarling, or you hit him right between the eyes."

Margaret was prevented from answering by a deafening roar from outside which told them, without doubt, that Jan Schroeder had brought his car to the front door, and he entered in much the same manner.

"I have come to offer you a lift back to your hotel," he said to the English girl. "After the perils of your pedal-pushing machine you'll be as safe as houses in my Lotus. I can tell you the arrangements for the flight as we go."

While Margaret got to her feet and collected her handbag, Jan took Helen's hands and gave her a resigned look. "Every time I come here I seem to shatter the calm peace of this place. I think I had better keep away."

"Jan," she said firmly, "I am past the stage of being taken in by your considerable charm. After nine years of Schroeders, I am beginning to be impervious to their wiles. There is no intention on your part to stay away. You just want to hear me claim that I couldn't do without your visits." His grin confirmed her words and she shook her hands free. "*I* know that Margaret will be perfectly safe in an aircraft with you, but please drive that car of yours at less than half your normal speed or *she* will never believe it."

Goodbyes were said on the *stoep* once

more, and if it hadn't been for the men's set faces, it would have been difficult to believe there had been such high tension a short time ago. Helen wished the other girl a successful stay at the Game Reserve, and promised to write. Chris added his words to that and told her that Jan would explain the altered flight arrangements.

"I'll see you at the airport," he called as the engine roared into life and Jan did the graceful driveway full justice with his tight turn and smooth get away.

The Lotus might be a "danger-machine" as Chris had named it, but Margaret had to admire the way it was handled. The speed must have been more than half his usual rate, but she felt perfectly safe as they wound their way along the coast to her hotel. What she had condemned during her cycle ride now seemed the best and most exciting way to travel, and a smile played on her lips as she threw back her head to let the breeze rush through her hair.

Jan spoke suddenly. "How about having dinner with me tonight? I do owe you some compensation for this afternoon."

"You make it sound like an insurance payment, but I'll accept, just the same."

24

"Good. Be ready at nine. I'll have that pedal-pusher repaired, for what good it may do you."

"I'm planning to take it to Myala. It might come in useful for getting about."

He flashed her a look with high amusement in his light brown eyes. "Cycling in a Game Reserve might be excellent for the health but very tough on the behind. There are only rough tracks leading from one place to another. I can see this evening will be spent in educating you on life in a place like that. Should prove interesting," he added to himself.

Margaret watched him as he turned into Plein Street and moved into heavier traffic. His face was still very freckled beneath his tan, and the bright hair still curled flat against his head in a cut which was probably not much different from the one he had had as a boy—but he had come a long way since then! Maybe she couldn't catch a lion by the mane, or hit him right between the eyes, but she was very experienced at anaesthetizing wild creatures until they learned to accept her!

He let her out at the hotel entrance and

re-affirmed his intention to collect her in just over three hours.

"I'll be ready," she promised, then hesitated. "I'm sorry you met with such opposition this afternoon. I thought Chris was rather unreasonable."

"Not at all. He hasn't seen the Dakota; I have. It was a natural enough reaction. I would have done the same in his place. Tot Siens," he added, and roared away. It was her first experience of the Schroeders closing ranks against outsiders.

The thought of an intimate dinner on a balcony overlooking a bay was killed almost before it was born. They had just set off when Jan apologized for having to make a very brief business call first. They followed the coastal road for some time, which gave Margaret another opportunity to see the really splendid scenic qualities of this peninsular. When she was wishing it would go on and on, Jan turned off and soon entered the forecourt of a very ugly modern mansion. Margaret waited in the car while her companion went in, but he soon reappeared and walked round to open her door.

"There is a party starting and we are

26

invited." He took her arm to help her out. "When Van Heerdon throws a party it's really something. You'll get more to eat here than I could have bought you at the Golden Bay hotel."

Margaret had no wish to attend a party given by the dubious Van Heerdon, but Jan was apparently a dab hand at *faits accomplis* and she was inside the house handing her coat to a coloured maid before a suitable comment occurred to her.

Her host, short, thickset and sandy-haired, summed her up optically as he approached and apparently found she reached his required standard. A smile altered the rather severe pale face as introductions were made, but it was his voice which surprised her. With a name like Van Heerdon, it was reasonable to suppose his English would be accented in the way of most people she had met in Cape Town, but he spoke in an upstage Etonian drawl which may have fooled South Africans, but to Margaret sounded as phoney as vinyl masquerading as leather.

The room was already filling up and Jan was immediately set upon by two girls who declared he simply must demonstrate a particular trick they had been describing to a man called Sammy. Before he allowed himself to be dragged off, Jan introduced Margaret as Maggie Ward, a friend of his sister-in-law. The two girls showed quite openly that they had not for one minute believed she was a friend of Jan's and Margaret smiled inwardly. She was used to that kind of look from board-thin jetsetters with orange mouths, carefully streaked hair, and earrings which reached to their shoulders, but there was no shortage of men who found her own glowing complexion, dark glossy hair, and very rounded curves infinitely preferable.

This was not her scene at all, but she found an evening spent this way provided her with an interesting study of human nature. Indeed, Jan was now the centre of a rowdy group who were urging him on to balance six full glasses, one on top of the other, on his chest as he bent backwards. He wore the right uniform—skintight white trousers and an orange shirt fastened at the neck with a patterned scarf—but Margaret felt sure this was not his scene either. Just why did he do it?

Van Heerdon, completely forgotten by

the English girl, followed her eyes and remarked into her ear, "That's why I like him. He is very malleable."

"I don't agree," she flashed back. "Adaptability is vastly different from weakness. I envy him his capacity to change from shrewd company director to light-hearted guest within a couple of hours."

"You've not known him long, I take it, Maggie," he said, using the ridiculous diminutive Jan had given her, "because you are from the 'mother country' as they say in the colonies. Let's make ourselves comfortable while you tell me how you met him."

He led the way to a purple and white striped sofa by a vast window and provided her with a tomato juice before sitting beside her. "Jan is so casual, he didn't give a hint of your relationship beyond your being a friend of Helen. Are you staying with her?"

She shook her head. "Jan is flying me up to Myala on Wednesday. I have been lucky enough to get an invitation from Russell Martin to further my ecological studies there. I am a fully-qualified vet but England is a bit restrictive when it comes to specialized study. Doctor Martin asked the Schroeders to fly me up when they took the supplies. That's as far as my knowledge of the family extends."

"Yet you make instant character analyses! I'm always a little resentful when a woman hides a shrewd brain behind an ultra-feminine exterior. I feel she is taking unfair advantage." The smile hardly matched the soft tone of his voice.

"Come, Mr. Van Heerdon, women have been liberated long enough to make a remark like that completely redundant. And surely, if a man's conscience is clear, he has nothing to fear from a woman."

"Please call me Elliot—everyone does. I like you, Maggie, but you frighten me somewhat. I have the uncomfortable impression that I might easily underrate you."

"Why 'uncomfortable'?" she asked him, disliking the man more every minute.

He took a draught from his glass while his pale eyes tried to make her break her steady gaze. He didn't succeed. "I prefer to deal with people who are transparent. I know exactly where I stand, then. Take Jan, for instance. He is motivated by the desire to take possession of Schroeder

Freight limited. For that he needs money and is prepared to do anything to get it. That's what I meant when I said he is malleable."

"You are wrong," Margaret told him. "The tip of an iceberg may seem transparent, but it is an elaborate trick to hide the opaque mass beneath the sea."

He tilted back his head in a supreme gesture. "I know Jan Schroeder. I can buy him any time I like."

2

THE evening dragged on. It was only made bearable for Margaret by the company of a Dutch mining engineer who told her about his experiences in the various diamond mines in the country. He had an amusing way of telling the most ordinary details which enchanted her and brought a sparkle to her eyes. Dancing had begun some time earlier and she had watched Jan shuffle round the room with a succession of melting girls held tightly against him while he laughed down into their eyes. It was all a sham! At the end of each dance, they took other partners and behaved in exactly the same way.

Eventually, he came across to break the mining engineer's monopoly saying, "You have been chatting up the girl I brought to this party for far too long. If you have no intention of dancing with her, I will."

They had hardly reached the clear space in the centre of the room when Margaret said, "I'd really prefer to go home. Could you call me a taxi?"

"Not on your life," he replied. "We'll have this one dance, then I'll drive you back."

"There's no need for you to do that. I don't want to stop your enjoyment."

He gathered her against him. "Whatever makes you think I was enjoying myself?"

"But . . ."

"Shh!" he said. "There are times when women should be held and not heard."

It was beautifully peaceful out in the dark night. They walked to the car side by side, their footsteps ringing in the silence. Margaret breathed in the fresh air gladly and remarked on what a relief it was to get out from the smoke-filled atmosphere.

"I noticed you were drinking tomato juice in there. Putting two and two together, I'd say you were an advocate of good, clean living. Am I right?" he asked.

She slid into the car. "There's no need to make it sound so dismal! What really annoys me is that you smoke, drink and generally flout all the rules of the game, yet manage to remain as fit and healthy as I am. There is no justice in the world."

He laughed softly. "Poor Maggie! I suppose you'll ditch that pedal-machine now. After all, why deprive yourself when you can achieve the same object by indulgence and dissolution!"

They set off at breakneck speed which dispelled all remnants of stale smoke and stuffiness.

"Are you very friendly with our host of this evening?" she asked out of the blue.

"Not a bit. He is a business associate, not a friend. Why?"

"Chris said he is a crook, but you couldn't see it. Is he right?"

"About Van Heerdon being a crook . . . yes."

That surprised her. "Then why do you deal with him?"

"Because it suits my purpose at the moment." He swung round a sharp bend and Margaret was thrown against him. When she straightened up she confronted him with, "Do you really aim to take over Schroeder Freight? Van Heerdon says you do."

"Then he should keep his observations to himself. Why the great interest in my business dealings? You are not planning on becoming a tycoon, are you?"

She ignored that. "The Dakota he sold you . . . is it any good?"

He laughed again. "Oh my, oh my! Not another one doubting my knowledge of aircraft. It's becoming an epidemic."

"Is it any good?" she persisted.

"Yes, my lovely, she is a bargain. That's why I bought her. Compared with our other machines you would hardly say this Dakota is a queen, but she is solid and reliable. I have been anxious to lay my hands on one for a long time. The company needs a stand-by aircraft in case one is put out of action. This Dak fits the bill admirably and has only cost us a third of what we would pay for any other. She's one of the early models but everything is in the right place, and tomorrow I plan to go over her from nose to tail. Our flight to Myala will be smooth and safe. I can't offer you first-class comfort, but no doubt you will relish the Spartan conditions."

She smiled. "And all because of a bicycle and glass of tomato juice! Would it astonish you to know I have an electric blanket to warm my bed in winter?"

"I can think of more exciting alternatives," he said dryly. "Does it really get that cold?"

"Where I come from it does." She didn't elaborate because at that moment the car turned on to a road skirting a bay and the full beauty of the starlit night drove all conversation from her.

Far out to sea, a liner edged its way into the harbour, the lighted portholes giving the impression of a giant, floating honeycomb, and in the foreground breakers crashed on to the beach in oblique lines, filling the night with the exciting sound of water assaulting land. There were still people on the beach. Margaret could see groups of young people in brief swimsuits, their brown bodies gilded by lights from the road, some lying around idly chatting and some using a ball-game as an excuse to indulge in a battle of the sexes with the girls as delighted losers. Jan swung round a wide curve and brought Margaret back to an awareness of unfamiliar surroundings.

"Where are we?" she asked.

"Our plans were somewhat interrupted by the party, so I thought we'd go back to my flat for a quiet drink," Jan told her.

And that's *all*, she added silently, used to the capers she was expected to take part in in these situations. On the other hand, she was glad the evening had not fizzled out as she had thought. The flat was expensive, as Helen had indicated, but not as flamboyant as it could have been. He had used good sense and some small flair for colour to produce a surprising blend of comfort and decor in the main room. He took Margaret's coat and she made a bee-line for a chair which was designed for only one reasonably-sized person. A ghost of a grin touched his lips when he saw how firmly ensconced she was.

"In the light of your disillusionment tonight, may I pour you something other than tomato juice?"

"Yes, I'd love some coffee," she replied. "Is that asking too much?"

"Heaven preserve me from a teetotal woman," he groaned. "You'll have to make it yourself, Maggie. Come on, I'll show you where everything is."

It may have been his way of getting her out of that chair but, as the kitchen was not very orderly, she was glad of his company to ease the job of searching for things. While the coffee was being prepared she asked him about the Game Reserve where she was to work for the next six months—maybe more. Schroeder Freight Limited had been flying supplies up to Myala and transporting live animals from there to zoos, or to the international airports and docks for shipment overseas, and both brothers knew Russell Martin well. Since Margaret was to be under his direction, she was curious about what type of man he was.

"I can only tell you my impression of him as a person. The research he does, or how far he is prepared to help you with your work, you'll have to find out for yourself. Chris used to fly animals for him before I ever joined the company, and he remained faithful to Schroeder Freight even when Chris went bust nine years ago. I think that fact is an excellent pointer to his character—loyal, sincere, stands by his beliefs. The Reserve has been under his direction for fifteen years or more, which means he is more at home with animals than he is with humans. He says he feels a special affinity with them. I must say he handles them expertly."

"There is no Mrs. Russell, then?"

Jan shook his head. "If there had been, she would have left him years ago. I never knew a man more cut off from the rest of the world by his work." He held the door open for her to pass through with the tray. "You have nothing to fear from him, but watch your step with his assistant, Craig Barker. He is a real lusty fellow. It's beyond me why a girl like you should want to bury herself up there amongst a lot of animals." He followed her as she carried the tray in and set it on a low table.

When she turned round to answer him and found herself in his arms, she could only marvel that she had fallen for such an old trick. The kiss was as she knew it would be: expert, very insistent and designed to arouse any woman between sixteen and sixty. On guard since she crossed the threshold, her immediate reaction was to let herself go completely limp and lifeless. He lifted his head abruptly and stepped back with an intuitive smile.

"I was expecting a struggle, or a slapped face."

She shook her head. "Experience has taught me that both those reactions only urge a man on—especially if he has been drinking. There is nothing more fatal to the natural urges of the male of the species than complete indifference—or a bucket of cold water."

"My God!" he exploded, the smile vanishing. "You make me sound part of a biology lesson. Shouldn't you do a few diagrams on the blackboard, now?"

"See what I mean," she said calmly. "All desire to be amorous has gone. Shall we have our coffee?" As she sat in the chair designed for one he crossed to the bar and poured himself a drink.

"I have to hand it to you English girls," he said with his back to her. "You are the supremos when it comes to cool, dispassionate forbearance. Helen displays it, at times."

"It must be our cold climate," she said, suddenly less sure of herself.

"And the fact that you only have electric blankets to warm you in bed." He tossed back the drink and was refilling the glass when the telephone rang.

Margaret drank her coffee at the risk of scalding herself. She would leave after the phone call. Maybe she had gone too far, and it was now impossible to remain in each other's company. It was almost midnight and tiredness was creeping upon her, bringing with it a faint backache; a reminder that she had had a heavy fall earlier that day.

Jan's voice rose above her thoughts setting her curiosity alight. "What a bloody nerve! He had no right to do that . . . No, of course I'm not withdrawing from the deal. He didn't agree—I told you he wouldn't—but we thrashed it out this afternoon and it was agreed that I would pay for it myself . . . Let *me* worry about where the money is coming from, will you? The time to start jumping on me is when I don't produce the next payment . . . Yes, yes, I'm flying it to Myala on Wednesday, as arranged, and Chris can go to hell. He may be my older brother, but we have equal shares in this company—oh, and in future, don't check on me, Van Heerdon. We have done enough business together for you to know I keep my word, and if Chris tries anything like that again, hang up on him!"

Margaret had seen his anger that afternoon, but now he was livid with it. Hastily she collected her handbag and coat.

"I think I should go."

"Yes, I think you should," he agreed harshly. "I have had more than my daily quota of people telling me what I should, or should not do." He picked up the car keys from the sideboard.

"I'll take a taxi. There is no need for you to drive me home."

"I know, but I am taking you just the same. I can see through you, Miss Biology Teacher. Your intelligent scientific mind is telling you that this particular male of the species is possibly slightly tight and definitely raging mad—a state incompatible with driving a fast car. I shall now prove to you that the theory is wrong and give teacher a rap over the knuckles." He grabbed her arm and marched her down the corridor, into the lift and out to the car without another word.

If his intention had been to frighten Margaret, it failed. Certainly, he had been drinking, but to someone used to consuming alcohol the amount had been no more than he could handle, and his anger was controlled to do more damage to his nervous system than his car. The journey was swift and silent, but Margaret sat there, feeling immensely sorry for him.

From the telephone conversation, it seemed Chris had gone behind Jan's back to tell Van Heerdon the Dakota deal was off; a move sure to inflame the younger Schroeder. The motives for Chris's action might have been of the purest, but the method had resulted in Jan being forced to defend his business integrity to a man he didn't like. She could sympathize with how he felt and regretted her own rather juvenile behaviour. Here, maybe, was one wild creature who refused to be anaesthetized; who needed special handling by someone who completely understood his complex nature!

Wednesday morning dawned magnificently. Table Mountain stood great and grey behind the city which Margaret already felt loath to leave. As a rule, she much preferred rural areas, but Cape Town had captivated her as soon as she arrived ten days ago. The final look from her bedroom window made her almost regret the necessity of flying up to the Game

Reserve. The sun-washed, tree-lined streets had a foreign flavour which pleased her each time she strolled through them, and whichever way she turned there was either a view of the marine blue ocean or the silver grey rock-faces of the mountains which cupped the city as a child's hand protects his answers on an examination paper.

Having come straight from Norfolk in December, Margaret was specially conscious of the sun-browned, healthy inhabitants and couldn't help comparing them with the careworn, head-scarved women who were shrammed with cold as they finished their Christmas shopping at home. She had probably looked the same way herself a mere fortnight ago. No wonder Helen had thought the world well lost to settle in this spot with a man like Chris Schroeder! That brought her thoughts back to his brother and she turned away with a sigh to go down to the lobby.

Jan looked very businesslike when she met him at the airport; the flashy silk shirt had been replaced by a khaki bush jacket and his trousers, though just as tight-fitting, were also in serviceable khaki.

44

"Is this all you've got?" He indicated her luggage with a nod of his head.

"Yes. Although they delivered the bicycle fully repaired, I decided against taking it. I can always do exercises to keep fit."

They entered the Dakota through a door near the tail, and Jan had to put his hands on her waist to push her up to the lowest step of the metal ladder he had hooked into the opening. After the jetliner in which she had travelled to South Africa, Margaret had to admit this aircraft was a Cinderella, and wondered if Chris could have been right when he called it a heap of scrap-iron. As she walked up the steep slope of the stark shell forming the freight hold she remembered Jan's warning that she would have no first-class comfort on this flight.

The cockpit was reached through a thick door and Margaret felt as if she had walked on to the set of a wartime film. The mass of controls, dials and levers looked quite familiar and only needed four dashing young men in leather flying helmets, giving the thumbs-up signal, to complete the illusion.

"You'd better sit there. I can't have you

in the co-pilot's seat. You might touch the controls." Jan's voice broke across her visions of Kenneth More and Richard Attenborough, but she was quick enough to retort, "I am quite able to resist the urge to push knobs and turn handles!"

"Look," he said, "you have your rules when it comes to experiments with the human male; I have mine when I am flying. All the time we are in this machine, you do whatever you are told. Is that clear?"

"Yes, quite!"

"Sit down and fasten that belt around you, then keep quiet until we are off the ground."

"Roger, skipper," she found herself saying, but Jan didn't think it funny and the need to hold back a smile soon vanished.

Her padded seat was tucked into a little cubby-hole with a table-top before it and a narrow window giving her a view of the port-side wing and propeller. She sat down and fastened the belt with some misgivings. From this position, the pilot was hidden, making her feel uncomfortably cut-off. Also, the Dakota was bigger than she had imagined and faint anxiety about Jan's ability to fly such an aircraft on his own made her wish she could watch what he was doing in order to take her mind off things.

The engines made a deafening roar! It was all right for Jan, he had earphones on and was exchanging take-off instructions with the control tower so, presumably, it was slightly reduced, but Margaret wondered how she would ever stand the din for five hours. They taxied forward to reach the runway and were just slewing round to face the long, straight stretch when she noticed a car racing towards them from the hangar marked *Schroeder Freight Ltd*. She undid her seat-belt and walked up behind the pilot.

"There is someone driving after us. Hadn't you better stop?" she shouted at him.

"Can't," he told her over his shoulder. "I'll lose my place in the queue. Now, for God's sake sit down as I ordered you ten minutes ago!"

"I can't see anything when I'm sitting down," she complained, but did as he asked. Immediately, the engine noise increased, there was a forward jerk which sent her pressing back into her seat, and the Dakota rumbled into a remarkably short take-off which might not have been the smoothest Jan had ever made, but was certainly the hastiest. The comparatively unfamiliar controls didn't hold his attention exclusively, so he found time to laugh softly to himself.

Margaret sat worrying over what she had seen, but had more sense than to bother Jan now. Her limited knowledge of flying was sufficient to tell her that it was impossible to stop in the middle of a take-off. He would have to circle the airfield then put down again once he realized the situation. The awful sensation of the roof pressing on her head lessened the higher they climbed, but the beauty of Cape Town below went unnoticed.

As soon as Jan stopped speaking into the mouthpiece attached to the earphones, Margaret leant out and caught his attention.

"Your brother Chris was in that car."

"So I saw!"

"Well . . . it must be important. Shouldn't you go back?"

"I know what he wanted."

"You know?"

He grinned broadly. "I can make a pretty good guess. To break my neck, I shouldn't wonder."

"You are not making sense."

He pushed back the headphones and laughed gaily. "I have just pulled a fast one on dear brother, and he won't like it a bit. He flatly refused to let me take you to Myala in this and was all set to make a diversion on his way to Kimberley in the Trilander. It seemed complete nonsense for both of us to go to Myala, but the situation was so tense, it seemed the only way to calm him down last Monday. I was all set to tell you the altered arrangements when Van Heerdon telephoned with the information that Chris tried to cancel the purchase of the Dakota without telling me. Because of that, I decided to let things stand and whisk you away from under his nose. I deliberately left the timing a little tight, but it couldn't have been better."

Margaret felt all churned up. Jan was treating her as a pawn in a game of one-upmanship. There was no question of flying a paying passenger to a required destination; she had been used merely as a means of getting at Chris. She now remembered Chris calling from the *stoep*, "See you at the airfield." He might think she had been a willing participant in this outrageous trip. Really, this red-haired man was impossible, as Helen had said!

"For a man of twenty-eight, you behave in a remarkably juvenile manner," she flung at him.

"So I am constantly being told—but since they are all older than I, it's hardly surprising they look at it that way."

"I assume you are referring to your brothers. Isn't it time you stopped playing adolescent pranks on them?"

"For a foreigner, you have a hell of a nerve when it comes to interfering in my affairs," he blazed. "This is no adolescent prank. It was damned ridiculous for two of us to fly to the same place just because Chris thought this aircraft too unsafe to risk your lovely skin. Do you think *I'd* fly it if it was? And when it comes to juvenile behaviour, brother Chris runs a close second by trying to ruin a good business deal by going behind my back—and *he* is thirty-seven."

Continued conversation was impossible.

They both retired into an aggrieved silence which went on so long there seemed no way of breaking it. It was hot inside the cockpit. Margaret took a cologne flagon from her handbag and rubbed some over her forehead, behind her ears and on her wrists. Her feet in their sandals were swollen, and the broad straps clung to her damp skin uncomfortably. The dress which had seemed pleasantly cool earlier this morning had grown warmer, and her hair which hung to her shoulders before turning under clung to her neck like a fur scarf. She pushed it up with her hands and leant her head back trying to get comfortable. The lack of contact with the only other person present left her with time hanging heavily. She read the various notices twenty-five times, decided it was impossible to see anything from the window, and searched through her handbag on four different occasions, then found the noisy drone of the engines was beginning to give her a headache. She looked at her watch. Only an hour had passed. It seemed like four!

She tried to concentrate on what she would be doing at Myala, but enthusiasm refused to be aroused. It was surprising.

For months, every time she had thought about being in Africa observing the wildlife in its natural environment, a small flutter of excitement had moved inside her. It had been a great stroke of luck that she had attended a party and met a man who had a friend in Africa working on a Game Reserve. Life had been like that for her. Things had come easily. She had been blessed with brains and intelligence enough to enable her to follow the career she most wanted, and she had passed her examinations with distinction.

When she had first qualified she was offered a coveted post at the Institute of Animal Sciences so that she could concentrate on a study of ecology—the branch which fascinated her most—but her dominant interest in African animals had to be confined to studying data from zoos and safari parks in England until her chance meeting with the man who had started her off on this trip. Where some people waited years for an opportunity of this kind, it had dropped into her lap like a sun-ripened orange. There would be six months—maybe more, if she could get round Dr. Martin—in which to saturate her brain with a fascinating study before returning to England.

The turn her career might take at that stage was too far ahead for her to plan, but the last two days had brought the Schroeder family on to her horizon with such impact it had unsettled her contentment. It would take a little while before she could put them out of her mind and settle in her temporary home!

Violent jerking and shaking brought Margaret from her doze. It was dark and rain was battling against the fuselage like the sound of Chinese crackers. A giant plunge threw her back into a reclining position as she was struggling to sit up, and a wave of nausea rose in her throat. Her handbag dropped to the floor as they tilted steeply before rising as quickly as they had dropped, and she automatically got up to retrieve the bag. The movement caught the tail of Jan's eye. He cast a quick glance her way and shouted, "We've hit a bad storm. I'm trying to get above it but she's rather sluggish. Get yourself strapped into the seat, and don't panic."

"I'm not panicking, but I feel slightly sick."

"Concentrate on something else," he advised unsympathetically.

She tried reading the notices once again, but every lurch brought a return of the feeling and she began to dread the worst!

Jan had plenty to occupy his mind during the aerobatics. It was just his luck to hit a storm of this magnitude when he was flying an unfamiliar machine. Normally he would have been out of it by now, but the Dakota, solid and dependable as she was, was a bit slow in responding and he had miscalculated several manoeuvres already. They were well into the heart of the storm and, with luck, had survived the worst. He sincerely hoped the girl behind him was not going to succumb to air-sickness. Although he felt the experience would do her good, they had another hour ahead of them yet and she had annoyed him enough on this trip as it was. He wished Chris were with him to see the way this old lady of an aircraft was coping with her battering. It would prove he was right to buy her. His lips tightened. Why should he have to prove he was right! Chris should accept his word.

Margaret was feeling extremely miserable. Another sudden drop brought sweat to her brow and increased her desire to reach her handbag which was sliding back and forth along the floor. In it were some smelling salts which would alleviate the faintness she was beginning to feel. It was an emergency which, she felt, justified unstrapping the seat belt and making a bid to reach the ubiquitous handbag. It was a rather shaky girl who got to her feet and took the three steps to where it had become wedged. Jan noticed the movement and turned his head.

"I told you to stop where you were," he yelled, but the end of the sentence was broken by a deafening crack as lightning hit the nose of the plane and ran over the fuselage until it met the wing. The electric charge brought an eerie whistling sound as it zig-zagged its way across the metal, then it hit the starboard propeller. A blinding flash, a tilt to port, and Jan knew the worst.

There was a range of mountains ahead and with one engine gone he would never gain enough height to clear them. Calmly he checked with Johannesburg met. men as to how far the storm extended and was told it covered the mountains at present, but was moving very rapidly. It should be clear when he approached. He thanked them and signed off. There was a choice— go on and make a wide detour to avoid the highest point in the range, or divert to Johannesburg. He had just decided the latter would be feeble when, next minute, there was *no* choice!

They were riding-out the outer fringe of the storm where the turbulence was worst, and two quick buffets in succession took the Dakota broadsides. By the time Jan had fought to keep the machine flying on course they had dropped too low. The remaining engine was in the twilight of its life, so they began a gradual let-down.

"What is happening?" called Margaret, her sickness banished by fright. "Is it out of control?"

"Not on your life," he snapped. "Get back in that seat."

"I have a right to know what is wrong with this aircraft," she said, standing firm. "Are we going to crash?"

"We are going to land, and if you'll shut up I'll try to work out where we are. There's no danger. It's not the first time I have put down without a runway, but I'd rather choose my spot if I can. Now, fasten your belt, and when I shout, cover your head with your arms."

She went back to her seat on shaking legs. Van Heerdon *had* sold him a pup, and it was being proved in the most dramatic way. All his brave talk of superior knowledge had been the immature bragging of a man unsure of himself!

The sound of rain was deafening and every wobble, every lurch, set her heart thudding anew. It would have been better to have occupied the other seat beside Jan. At least she would know when they were about to hit the ground. In this cubby-hole, she was as cut-off from him as if she had been a passenger in a commercial aircraft. Sudden pressure on top of her head indicated that the angle of descent had increased, the remaining engine ground out an agonized roar, and a gigantic hand seemed to have taken hold of the tail, holding the aircraft back as it struggled to get free.

"*Head down!*" yelled Jan, and she doubled forward into a tight ball as a weird screeching and rattling began. The whole fuselage shook as it thumped on to the ground, rose again, then landed with a bigger jolt which shook and shuddered the machine from nose to tail as they rushed headlong across the uneven *veld* to end with a dizzy swing amid high-pitched shrieks.

The deathly hush which followed went on and on, broken only by the hammer of rain. She might have been the only living thing on earth as she hugged herself and waited for an explosion which didn't come.

"Jan," she cried. "Jan . . . are you there?"

Silence! Dear God, she thought, whatever has happened!

Her legs were not up to taking her weight just yet so she crawled forward to the flight cabin and found Jan slumped to one side, out cold. Beside him, the fuselage had caved in, trapping his left leg beneath a jagged piece of metal which was cutting deeply into his flesh. Blood soaked into the khaki material of his trousers in sufficient quantities to convince the girl that something must be done, and quickly. Professional competence banished all emotion as she searched for a medical box, praying that Jan had ensured it was complete before setting off. She found it wedged between the back of the seat and a bulkhead . . . and it was full. He earned top marks for that.

It proved impossible to move him. He was a big man and the space was so confined she realized that the only way to staunch the bleeding would be to climb over his knees and treat the wound as best she could. Once she had administered emergency measures, she could afford the time to think of a way to release him. Hastily she unpacked some of her under-clothes to make a thick pad to press on the wound, then started to edge her way between the pilot's seat and the control column which rose up between the two seats.

It was tricky. Progress was halted half-way when her skirt caught on a lever behind her, and with her hands full and her legs astride him, she had to twist round to try to release it with her elbow. For several seconds, it was a vain task and her foot slipped against a lever lying along the floor. It sprang up and next minute, the whole aircraft collapsed beneath her and sent her sprawling across Jan's lap. For the next thirty seconds she waited for an explosion, but once it had settled raindrops made the only break in the silence, as before.

She struggled to her feet, half-expecting the floor to drop further, but the Dakota seemed to have made herself comfortable now. The movement proved advantageous. The side of the cockpit had been twisted upwards to a certain extent making it possible for her to release Jan's leg from the jagged edge which had caused all the trouble. The gash was deep and needed stitching. Making a shortie nightie into a pad with some of the wadding from the medical kit, she pressed it against the freely bleeding wound and bound it tightly in place with a bandage. Then, she scrambled back to organize an injection of morphia which was also in the box. He would need it when he came round!

As though he had read her thoughts, a low moan came from the pilot's seat and she glanced up from the task of filling the syringe from the small silver ampule.

"Keep still!" she directed him. "I'll be there in a moment."

The brown eyes were open but hazy with non-recognition when she approached.

"Are you capable of following what I say?" she asked.

"Eh?"

"I'm going to give you a shot of morphia to help deaden the pain, then I want you to try, with my assistance, to move from there on to the floor. What do you think?"

"Go ahead," he invited from his slumped position.

Once more she began climbing over the mass of controls to reach him, half-afraid of being sent flying as before. Jan had moved his head since he came round, revealing another wound to the side of his skull. She would have to attend to that when he was on the floor. She reached him and carefully unbuttoned the bush jacket, pulling it from his right shoulder to get at the top of his arm. His body was hard and brown from the African sun.

"I must warn you that I usually only administer injections to dogs and cattle—but I dare say it is much the same for a man," she said lightly.

"Thanks." He flinched from the jab she gave his muscle and sighed with relief when she withdrew the needle. "Pity the cattle," he murmured.

"Thank your lucky stars you are sitting down. It is usual to inject morphia in the buttocks," she told him tartly as she pulled the jacket across him. "Now we'll try to get you on your feet." She slid an arm behind him. "Can you sit forward?"

"Not with you hanging over me in that seductive manner. Move over and I'll see what I can do on my own."

Not very much, as it turned out. He got as far as sitting straight, but as soon as his legs took his weight the pain from his thigh made him yell heartily and fall back again.

"We'll try it together, shall we?" Margaret said with the patience of a nannie to a fractious child.

It wasn't easy. Jan found every movement brought an agony he could scarcely withstand, and Margaret was not tough enough to bear his weight as he leant heavily on her shoulder. The worst part was getting him free from the controls, and both of them found it heavy-going. Once that was over, it was comparatively simple to settle him on the floor with Margaret's coat providing a pillow while she cleaned the area round the head wound.

The effort had taken a great deal out of him. Although he hadn't uttered a sound, the pallor of his face emphasized the liberal peppering of freckles more than usual, and Margaret had a fleeting return of her vision of a small boy defying his brothers by hiding his fear of being hurt. Then her lips clamped together. This time, he had only himself to blame for flying this old aircraft against all advice, simply to prove a point.

He asked her for a cigarette, but she told him with the carelessness of the non-smoker that he would have to wait until she had finished all she had to do. By the time a bandage was bound round the bright red hair, Jan's jacket was soaked with sweat which also stood out on his forehead. She took a towel from one of her suitcases and got busy on him despite his feeble protests. After that, she replaced the pad on his thigh which had become saturated during the struggle from seat to floor.

Attending to the injured man had driven every other thought from her head, but when she at last sat back on her heels, realization rushed in. Raindrops no longer beat a tattoo on the metal. The utter silence frightened her. Suddenly, the confines of this stark metallic tube brought an attack of claustrophobia, making the sweat stand on her brow, too, and setting a pulse drumming in her ears. The complete solitariness of her position at last dawned on her. In which particular part of Africa was she? How far was it to the nearest town? Jan's leg needed stitching as soon as possible, but he would never manage to walk anywhere. The obvious solution was for her to go for help while the drug was keeping him quiet, but without knowing the area, it was out of the question.

A look from the window showed her what she was up against. Emptiness stretched into eternity. A vast haze hung several feet from the ground where the noonday sun burned into the wet earth vaporizing the rain before it had time to refresh the undergrowth. The storm had passed and blazing heat returned to assail the rugged *veld*. Far, far in the distance a mountain range rose like a dark cloud, but the remainder of the terrain was short grass broken by stony patches and clumps of trees. The Dakota had apparently hit one of these. Several beheaded trunks and a tangle of broken wood and leaves caught in the port propeller gave Margaret the clue.

Next minute, it seemed imperative to get in the open air. Being slowly cooked in a metal container was not a pleasant sensation and brought a return of panic. There was a door marked EMERGENCY EXIT right behind Jan's seat and she struggled to open it before she felt the sun strike her bare arms. Then she walked to the tail and opened the door they had used to enter in Cape Town.

The atmosphere outside was hot and airless, but the hemmed-in feeling retreated at the sight of so much space and she leant against the side of the Dakota, trying to steady herself. There was danger in panic. In time, help must come and it was imperative to keep a clear head until then. Forcing herself *not* to think of the consequences if they were not found, she set about making them both as comfortable as possible.

The morphia had deadened the pain enough to allow Jan to drift into a near-unconscious state, so since it was out of the question to get him outside into the shade of the trees, she did what she could to make him cool. The material of the left leg was hopelessly ripped, so she cut neatly round his trousers until they were a brief pair of shorts, then took off his desert boots and thick socks. It also seemed sensible to remove the drill bush jacket for the two-fold purpose of making him cooler and drying it out. At the end of the operation she sat back on her heels and wiped her wet brow with the towel, and as she did so, found unwelcome feminine admiration being wrung from her. Whatever her opinion of his character, stripped down to a pair of shorts, he was a fine-looking man!

The longing for drink began and she hurried to the wall outside the toilet where a container claimed to hold water. It was empty—a relic of the old days when this aircraft was in constant use. It was a sad blow, and thoughts of a long, cool drink began to plague her until she reasoned that Jan would surely have brought water as a regular precaution when flying over wild Africa. She returned to his side and noted, with alarm, that he was getting dangerously hot. He was too dopey to get any sense from him, so she started a determined search for any containers which might supply what they desperately needed. At last, in a corner, she spotted the vital cans and thankfully drank the warm liquid. Then, she swamped Jan with it so that he roused enough to enable her to give him a drink, too.

Time passed in a series of sessions. Ten minutes beneath the trees, ten minutes dousing Jan with water, ten minutes of trying to think of how they were going to get away alive. Soon afterwards, flies began to swarm in and buzzed in a revolting mass around the blood-soaked pad on the injured man's leg. Unable to bear the sight, she emptied one of her cases and opened it over the leg to form a cage which she covered with a dress. The other preventative measure she took was to light cigarette after cigarette from the packet in Jan's bush shirt and hope the smoke would discourage them. No doubt, he would go up in smoke himself when he discovered she had let his entire supply burn away in her hand, but she could deal with him when the time came!

Leaden hours passed and she began to have hallucinations. Twice she imagined voices outside, but by now the effort required to climb through the door was too much. She leant back against the metal wall and studied Jan as her anger against him grew. Through his irresponsible behaviour she was stranded in the heart of Africa with a thin prospect of help arriving, and exposed to hazards of all kinds. He was strong, healthy, reasonably well-off and lucky enough to do what he most enjoyed as a means of earning a living. Many men would envy him—yet there was a restlessness raging inside that tanned breast which she didn't understand or condone.

She sighed. In England it would be cold . . . maybe snowing. Why had she ever left her homeland where life was organized and secure to cross a country like this in a broken-down aircraft flown by a wild South African? The soporific furnace she was in triumphed over her senses at around three-thirty, and she was still asleep beside the red-haired man when shadows fell across the doorway and two black Africans climbed in to reach her.

3

WHEN a hand shook her awake and held out a water bottle Margaret drank the lukewarm musky liquid instinctively, without seeing or caring who offered it. Jan's eyes were open and watching her.

"All right?" he asked faintly. "Don't worry about these fellows. They're here to help."

She looked up at the two black giants in khaki uniform who grinned like a pair of pianos. She thanked them, making their grins widen and their eyes roll, but they seemed shy of her and turned their attention back to Jan. After a short conversation in Afrikaans, the men walked to the back of the aircraft and began to unload the crates of supplies.

"Who are they?" asked Margaret thickly.

"Police on patrol. They get a lot of poachers in these parts. Good thing their route took them past here and they decided to investigate. I can't understand why we haven't been spotted from the air yet. It was difficult to give an accurate position in that storm, but I couldn't have been that much in error."

"You mean, somebody knew where we were?"

"Of course. It's standard procedure to radio your position when you know you're going to ditch. These men will take us to Alwynsrus, a small town about three hours' drive away and we can get a message to Myala from there. You can go on by road . . . it's not too far . . . and I'll radio Chris to fly up another engine for the Dakota. If he won't do it, I'll have to go back myself."

"Stop fretting about things like that," she told him, noticing how feverish he looked. "Your leg has to be stitched before you'll be capable of doing *anything*. Will there be a hospital at this place?"

"It's obvious you have never seen any of our towns."

"But there'll be a doctor?"

She didn't get the answer to that because the policemen indicated that they were ready to leave, and Margaret got to her feet to fetch the medical box.

"If you are going to be bumped and shaken over rough ground for the next few hours or so, I'll have to give you more morphia."

"Not another of those cattle injections!"

"How much pain can you stand?"

"All right, all right," he surrendered meekly, "but before you operate will you fetch my stuff from the cockpit? There's a canvas bag with the cargo manifest and all relevant documents. It also holds my pilot's licence, my wallet, and several other things I always carry with me."

She found the square satchel and put it with her handbag.

"You look pretty done-in," said Jan when she returned to him. "How are you feeling?"

"As well as can be expected," she replied shortly, taking the second ampoule from the box and filling the syringe before the goggling eyes of the policemen. They backed when she crossed to the man on the floor, bringing a faint smile to her face.

"What cowards men become when faced with a needle!" She squirted a little of the liquid into the air to test the syringe, then took his upper arm in her hand searching for the muscle.

"I assume it was you who undressed me," he murmured, "because care was taken to observe the proprieties."

The needle jabbed into his flesh bringing a tightening of his jaw and a martial look to her eye. "One of these men will help you to dress if you prefer it. *I* will renew the pad on your leg. That will be two nightdresses you owe me."

"You don't really wear those things, do you?" he taunted through gritted teeth. "In this country we sleep as nature made us."

She withdrew the needle angrily. "Nature hasn't made a very good job of you! This is not a jolly little adventure. While you have been sleeping-off the effects of that first dose, I have been alternately scared, roasted and parched. The next time you buy a white elephant which falls apart in mid-air, risk only your own neck, will you? I dare say I could sue you for taking me as a passenger against your partner's orders in a machine which was not airworthy."

He stared at her speechlessly for some

moments while a slow flush mounted his face, and his eyes hardened with anger.

"My God, that's what they'll all think! It will be their natural reaction." The handful of hair he clutched seemed in danger of being pulled from his scalp. "What a heaven-sent opportunity for them to preach and bring home long-standing charges of incompetence and irresponsibility! How they'll wallow in their self-righteous assertions that they knew all along that I would fly too high and come a cropper. And Chris . . . Chris will be magnanimous and offer to absorb some of my losses in the company funds, but I shall see the same look on his face as on all the others. It will be a complete waste of time to tell the truth. The odds against a plane's being struck by lightning are so high it would only increase their pity if I attempted to use it as an excuse for what happened." His eyes flayed her. "They brainwashed you well! You condemn me out of hand."

Margaret bent her head over the task of re-binding his leg wound but her hands began to shake. She hadn't known the reason for their forced landing, but he was right in believing she had had no faith in his judgement and too readily thought the worst of him. Her brave words to Helen that it was time somebody tried to understand him expressed a hollow intention, it now seemed. *Of course* Chris would never believe that the elements had played such a vicious trick on his brother, and Jan would not bother to convince him. This incident would be a fierce blow to his esteem and also his finances. He had impetuously vowed to pay for the Dakota himself —now he could add a repair bill to the price. All she had suffered was a few hours of discomfort, but he stood to lose face with his fellow-men, and most of his wealth . . . and she had accused him of thinking this a "jolly little adventure".

There seemed no way of bridging the gap caused by her accusation, so she remained silent instead of apologizing. He would not want her pity. She finished the bandage and helped him dress. The nights could be chilly, she knew. The Africans picked him up carefully and made their way through the fuselage towards the door with Margaret hovering beside them. She was impressing on them that the first essential was to get Jan to a hospital, and was so engrossed in this she missed the look which crossed Jan's face when they stepped to the ground.

"I don't believe it," he breathed, looking at the Dakota. "I didn't bring her in that way . . . I know I didn't. There's no way the . . ." He broke off and gave Margaret a sharp look. "Did you touch any of the controls?"

"I may have. My dress caught on a lever while I was climbing across to you and I had to fiddle with my elbows to try to release it. It wasn't easy with medical stuff in my hands, and to make matters worse, the plane suddenly collapsed. Have I done something?"

He didn't answer except to tell the Africans to carry on, but he closed his eyes as if in anguish and left Margaret to worry.

She didn't accept the offer to sit in the cab with the driver. One of them helped her into the back where they had laid Jan amongst the crates, and the truck set off. Although she had cushioned the leg with her clothes to protect it from the worst of the jolting, there was no doubt he was in considerable pain, at first. Mercifully, the morphia took over before they had been long on their way and Margaret was left to gaze from the back of the truck.

Soon, a cool breeze persuaded her to pull on a light coat and, in moving, she dropped the canvas satchel which Jan had asked her to bring. The flap opened, spilling the contents, and for several seconds papers flew about in the vortex until she and the policeman succeeded in catching them. The neatly-typed lists, folded documents and several licences in plastic covers didn't surprise her, but what did was a gun in a webbing belt, and a supply of bullets. The policeman examined the gun with professional curiosity, then handed it over, showing a flash of white teeth. Margaret put everything back in the satchel then locked it in one of her suitcases. It would be safer there.

Dark descended quickly. To Margaret it was a night of luminous stars and animal sounds which blended with weird dreams every time she dozed off so that, afterwards, she was never sure which was the sleeping or waking part. A terrible chill had invaded her bones and it set her teeth chattering. The temperature had dropped considerably, but it was more a fever brought on by her hours spent in the broiling heat of the aircraft than the coldness of the present. To a girl reared in Norfolk, an African night was not at all extreme.

A jolt brought her awake with a small cry. The night outside was broken by a pale halo of light which hung above a doorway in a low white-walled building. The policeman, who had travelled in the back of the truck with her, had jumped down and joined the driver who was pushing open the double doors. Clutching her coat around her she slid along the seat until she was peering round the edge of the canvas. An odour of antiseptic and a cross on the door told her they had reached a tiny hospital and she breathed her thanks to whoever was there to listen.

The policemen had an Indian in a white coat with them when they re-appeared, and he looked at the girl's face carefully before introducing himself in clipped English.

"Good evening. I am Doctor Gavascar . . . head of this clinic. I am told you require urgent treatment for your husband."

"Yes, he does need treatment . . . but

we are not related. He was flying me to Myala when we were brought down in a storm." She scrambled to the ground and smiled an apology. "Please forgive me, Doctor, but I don't seem able to collect my thoughts at present." She went on to describe Jan's injuries and how much morphia she had administered, until the doctor stopped her.

"But you surely do not need my help, madam. You have medical qualifications."

"Only for animals, unfortunately. This man's leg needs quite a few stitches in it, and he has already lost a lot of blood."

"I see," said the Indian thoughtfully. "I must warn you first that I have no white staff in my tiny clinic."

"You haven't?" said Margaret, quite missing the point.

"Your voice tells me that you are English. Is the pilot, also?"

"No, he is . . ." Rather late in the day she got the implication and flushed hotly. How long would it take her to get used to the ways of this country? She indicated the black policemen.

"When these two men turned up at the crash we were *both* very glad to see them and grateful for their help. I don't think the situation has changed in any way, Doctor Gavascar."

He gave her an understanding look. "Thank you, Miss . . . ?"

"Ward."

". . . Miss Ward. I will make arrangements to bring the patient in."

Jan was awake but vague as the stretcher men carried him into the building which, to Margaret, resembled not much more than the small utility extensions which were added to mansions in England during the war to house public offices. The floors were scrupulously clean and the tiny room into which Jan was taken held two hospital beds with white covers like the ones she had seen at home. Margaret followed automatically and stood beside the bed as though there were nothing strange about being there. Dr. Gavascar, recognizing a knowledgeable person when he met one, made no comment on her presence and set about instructing a Bantu nurse to uncover the wound.

The journey had done Jan no good. He was in a semi-comatose state and his cheeks had bright fever spots which flared beneath the dark-ringed eyes. There was no doubt the three-hour ride had taken its toll of his fortitude, and the anger brought on by her careless words to him had not helped to ease his mind. The doctor made arrangements to stitch up the gash at once, then he turned to Margaret.

"You look completely exhausted, dear lady, and somewhat feverish yourself. While I am dealing with this patient, a member of my staff will give you food and a sedative. In the morning you will feel better able to decide what to do."

A loud altercation appeared to be going on in the corridor, and an orderly burst in to explain the problem in a fast native language to the doctor. The difficulty was being caused by the crates which the policemen had started to unload into the clinic. There was just not room for them inside the building and Dr. Gavascar endorsed the orderly's warning about leaving them outside all night. Margaret was asked what the crates contained, but she merely knew Jan was delivering supplies to the Reserve. Whether it was food or veterinary supplies she couldn't say —probably both.

The situation reached a stalemate. Dr. Gavascar refused to have his corridor blocked by a dozen sizeable crates, yet would not take the responsibility of leaving them at the mercy of thieves outside. Margaret, conscious that Jan had already lost a valuable aircraft, felt extremely protective towards the cargo and insisted that the crates be put under lock and key somewhere, so with combined pressures being put upon them the policemen said they would convey the stuff to the police station in the town of Alwynsrus, five miles away. They then became adamant that the owner should go with them to fill in the necessary forms and accept a receipt. The sergeant would insist, they said.

Five minutes later, Margaret was back in the truck with the crates, bumping along the sand road to the police station. In view of Jan's condition, the policemen had reluctantly allowed her to take on the responsibility for the merchandise. They were plainly unhappy about the whole episode and sat in reassuring unity in the cab, leaving Margaret alone with her thoughts and a raging headache. Although she knew Jan was in good hands, a strange reluctance to leave him had invaded her the minute she knew she must go. Why had she not apologized for her doubts on his professional competence? Knowing how deeply affronted she would be if a layman had doubted her own ability in the field of animal medicine, she could at least have assured him she would support the truth about the cause of the accident. But then a man like Jan would not care to rely on a woman to convince his family of his worth. He would let them fling their opinions at him and say nothing.

The police station was not as large as the clinic, and was one of no more than a dozen buildings edging the road which formed the town. The word had naturally conjured up in Margaret's mind thoughts of neat rows of bungalows or houses, a shopping centre, hotels, and a population of at least several thousand. Alwynsrus, as far as she could see, was merely a hundred-yard stretch of road which provided the essentials needed for people passing through . . . but maybe darkness hid the remainder!

Inside, the bare walls and unscrubbed fustiness of the room showed her its official status as an office, but a door standing open at the far end allowed her a glimpse of house furniture and rugs on the floor. At a call from one of the Africans, scuffling was heard and a man's voice from the room caused the two black men to roll their eyes. Then the owner of the voice appeared at the doorway. He almost filled it! This man was as tall as the Schroeder brothers, but his girth was triple theirs. The waist-band of his trousers had to be content to lie below the spread of his stomach, which left his shirt buttons straining against his paunch without much success. Two were missing, and pale flesh was visible through the gap. He scratched at this gap with one hand while the other pushed greasy fair hair from his eyes.

"*Julle is laat!*" he accused the men and belched, then he saw Margaret. "*Wie is u?*"

"I beg your pardon?"

"Who the hell are you?"

"I might ask the same question. I was under the impression this was a police station." Her cool cultured tone made him flush with anger.

"English, are you? What do you want?"

The two Africans broke into a nervous

explanation, and the white man came further into the office as his interest grew. Margaret had a quick view of a woman's face peering from the room he had just left, and the little she saw persuaded her the woman was not his wife.

The policemen were despatched in no uncertain terms to bring in the crates and he turned to the girl. "They are lazy bastards at the best of times. What's in the boxes?"

"I'm afraid I don't know. The pilot has a cargo manifest with the rest of his papers. Supplies for Myala I was led to understand. Why?"

He shrugged his vast shoulders. "Curious, that's all."

Margaret found him difficult to understand. That thick Afrikaaner accent combined with a touch of alcoholic incoherence sounded like a foreign language to her dulled senses. As the crates were carried in he showed increased joviality, although he made no attempt to do any of the carrying. His manner changed from aggressive through conciliatory to downright pleasant, and the wide smile he eventually produced showed her he must have been a striking man not so many years ago. Now, he was in his forties—the prime of his life—and had let himself go to seed.

"Are you in charge?" Margaret asked.

"Have been for ten years. Sergeant De Wet is well-known around here—ask anybody." He leant towards her, expelling a beery gasp as his stomach was flattened against the desk. "When I first came, many people, including me, thought this was the end of the road. One little mistake . . . and a posting to a dump like Alwynsrus where I would serve out my time as a forgotten man. For several years I bore a grudge against the person responsible, until I discovered how rewarding a job like this can be. A man is his own boss out here. Like the local pastor, I have my flock and look after its interests. In a city I should be a mere Sergeant; here I am a Brigadier." His deep blue eyes sparkled with amusement. "Now you are part of my flock, so you had better tell me what you were doing in this freight aircraft."

"I am on my way to take up an appointment at Myala. I shall be studying there for the next six months, maybe more."

Sergeant De Wet leered. "*A flerric* like

you up there with Craig Barker! I can guess what you will be studying!"

Margaret assumed what Jan had called her cool, dispassionate forbearance, and asked whether she might have her receipt since the crates had all been unloaded. One of the Africans was entering details in a thick ledger; the other had disappeared. The blond sergeant pulled a scrap of paper towards him and scrawled a signature on it before handing it to the girl.

"There is nothing on here but a name," she protested.

"I can't state what I have received because none of us knows."

"I have no intention of accepting this as a receipt. Jan . . . Mr. Schroeder . . . would demand something more official."

The aggression was returning now. "Whether you accept it or not is up to you. I am not compelled to take those boxes in. I am doing it as a favour. Officially, I am off duty, so it is only because I live on the premises that you were not left to do what you could about this stuff." He cocked a thumb at the cargo. "I could remind you that the alternative would be to leave them at the mercy of *diewe*. There are plenty of them about in a country like this. They rise up out of nowhere, and the stuff vanishes into thin air."

"Despite the care the 'Brigadier' takes of his flock? You surprise me!"

Her taunt angered him further, and he turned on his heel, leaving Margaret standing with the paper in her hand. Jan would be furious! This signature meant nothing, but it looked as if she would have to take it or leave it. She waited until the African had finished writing in his ledger, but when he made no move, said. "Who will be driving me back to the clinic?"

He looked astonished. His clearly-defined duty had been to get a sick man to a hospital, then lock up some valuable items. This had been carried out to the letter. The sergeant had given no orders about the woman; she was no responsibility of his. Besides, he was now on the first shift of night-duty and unable to leave his post. He kept silent, hoping she would go away, but Margaret knew how to play the same game and they fought a battle of endurance. The African won. Behind him were generations of men who knew when it was best to keep a still tongue. Margaret in no way surrendered, however, she merely shifted her attack to a more familiar adversary.

"Sergeant," she called in a loud voice. "I am waiting for transport back to the clinic. Until you give the command, I imagine no one will make a move."

There was no reply from the room, so she knocked on the door and said, "As Brigadier of Alwynsrus do you think you could authorize one of these men to drive me five miles! I was in an air crash this morning, I have had nothing to eat all day . . . and if you don't do as I ask, I shall get into that truck and drive myself back."

That brought a bellow from within which sent the African running for the door. Within seconds, the other policeman appeared, rubbing his eyes, and climbed into the truck to start it up.

Dr. Gavascar was full of complaints about fussing over formalities when it was obvious she should be in bed. After a simple meal, during which she learned that Jan was now quite comfortable, the doctor bade her good night, and a nurse showed her where she could wash before handing over some tablets to help her sleep. Jan was dead to the world when she slipped into the bed opposite him, glad that the rules of this country made it necessary for them to share the same room. She felt a special responsibility for her first human patient.

For a long while, every time she closed her eyes, the bed became a police truck bumping over rough roads, or an aircraft being buffeted and tossed by storm winds. The tablets didn't have much effect on her bewildered brain which marched the day's events before her eyes in less than chronological order. Black faces and white faces swam above her like disembodied ghosts, some smiling, some threatening, but the one which plagued her most was covered in freckles and branded her as one who condemns without a trial. Eventually, sleep took over and she continued the theme through her dreams.

She was not the only one in that room who was wandering through time. In the early hours, Jan became restless and succeeded in waking Margaret with his noisy delirium. He was throwing his head from side to side while his hands clutched the cover convulsively. She heard Chris's name over and over again with parts of broken sentences which meant nothing to her, but she couldn't bear to let him continue. It took but a second to cross the room and take his hand. It was burning! She wiped the sweat from him with a small towel and spoke soothing words in the hope of calming him, but it was a vain task. At last, a Bantu nurse entered with her stately stride and took over where Margaret had failed. A couple of tablets, a small drink of water, and her patient was soon quietly asleep again, leaving the other occupant of the room gazing at the wall feeling distinctly melancholy. One phrase stood out in her mind and haunted her. "It hurt like hell, but I didn't holler, did I?" It was a man's body which had suffered, but the cry had come from a small boy. Who knew what was passing through his mind as he lay there.

It was light when she woke and found Jan looking at her.

"How are you feeling?" she asked immediately.

"Fine . . . just fine. You've had a hell of a time. I'm sorry."

"It wasn't a rave-up for you, either," she said, "but it could have been a lot worse, I suppose." Her head threatened to roll off her neck when she sat up, but a determined effort kept it upright while she poured water into a glass beside her bed. Jan's appearance cheered her. Apart from the reddish stubble and equally red-rimmed eyes which gave him a disreputable look, his colour was normal and his mind had returned from the past. He sat up carefully and reached across to his shirt lying folded on a table.

"Where are my cigarettes?" he asked after searching through every pocket.

"Burnt to smoke. I had to keep the flies away somehow."

"Hell! If ever I wanted one, it is now." He flung the shirt aside in disgust.

"Breakfast will do you more good," she told him cheerily. "What do they eat first thing in the morning in a place like this?"

"The same as at any other time of the day. It will be an unappetizing mess, I promise you." He was completely disgruntled now that he had been denied the one thing he most wanted. Margaret smiled to herself. "You'll eat it, just the same, or you'll be too weak to do anything."

He ran a hand through his hair. "Heaven

preserve me from 'nursy' types. I can't stand being treated like a difficult child. I like my women soft and submissive!"

"You won't be fit for any kind of woman unless you get some food inside you."

He gave her a long scowl. "Now I know why you became an animal doctor—they can't argue with the treatment."

To change the subject she asked, "Will you be able to get a message to Chris from here? If so, how long will it take him to get a new engine?"

"There's no point in worrying Chris," he said, looking carefully at the opposite wall. "I'm not sure the Dakota is worth saving."

She was astonished. "That's a complete reversal of what you said yesterday."

"At the time, I didn't realize the extent of the damage. I don't think I can afford the repairs, and Chris certainly won't sanction spending any money on it."

"I don't understand. How has the situation changed?"

The brown eyes swivelled to meet hers. "When we came down, I made a good landing—if we hadn't hit those trees in the blinding rain it would have been near perfect—but some time later the wheels folded up and she flopped on her belly. I can only guess that the locking gear was damaged on impact and you released the lever when you clambered over the controls." He paused. "Don't look so stricken!"

"But I feel responsible! Won't insurance cover the damage?"

"I . . . she was so damned cheap, our broker was hesitant over issuing a policy. I . . . well . . . I would have sorted the thing out when I got back." He plucked savagely at the coverlet. "I wasn't to know this would happen. You have to take risks in a business like ours or you lose clients."

"Would Chris have taken the risk?" Why had she said that? It was not like her to hit below the belt, but this man brought out a side of her character she had not known existed.

"No, he bloody-well wouldn't. You knew the answer before you asked the question, but if your object was to fill me with remorse, you failed. Given the same set of circumstances, I'd do it again."

Silence settled on the room. After breakfast Margaret gladly escaped to wash and dress in fresh clothes. When she returned, Jan had on the cut-off shorts and crumpled jacket, and had just finished washing in the bowl brought to his bedside. While putting her things back into her case Margaret came across the canvas satchel she had brought from the aircraft.

"Here . . . you had better take charge of this now." She tossed it on to his bed. "I don't know how much you remember of last night, but those policemen took me as far as the town so the crates could be locked in the police compound. They couldn't have all that blocking these corridors and it wasn't safe to leave it outside. The sergeant at the station didn't fill me with confidence. This is his idea of a receipt." She held out the scrap of paper. "He said it was impossible to state what he had received because nobody knew. I said I thought it was a mixture of food and veterinary supplies."

"That's about it," he confirmed. "I have the manifest here if he wants to see it. You seem to have handled my affairs with your usual competence, Maggie. You are putting me in a position no man likes to be in . . . but I'm very grateful." This was said stiffly and she guessed he didn't find it easy to accept. What had fostered this fierce independence of others this desire to head into the future knowing it was fatal trying to go it alone? Had he always shunned any suggestion of a helping hand?

She watched him as he sat on the bed putting his papers in order. A small dressing covered the head wound and his thigh was expertly bandaged, but the droop of his shoulders showed he was far from fit. A sudden clamour from outside brought his head up, and next minute, the door crashed open, making Margaret jump. Sergeant De Wet pushed between Dr. Gavascar and a nurse to command the centre of the room. One of the African constables covered the doorway, looking scared. The massive sergeant had his revolver pointing straight at Jan.

"On your feet!" he commanded.

"What the . . . !" exclaimed Jan angrily.

"Don't attempt to reach for your gun," he said, advancing and pulling out handcuffs. "You are under arrest."

"Don't be bloody stupid!" shouted Jan as the sergeant snapped them on his wrists and hauled him to his feet. "You can't arrest a man without cause."

"I am perfectly aware of my duties, man," was the answer.

Margaret stood up, trembling. "Take your hands off him! He has twenty stitches in his leg and has lost a lot of blood. Do you want to make him ill?"

"You keep out of this," Jan told her savagely as he leant against the bed-rail for support. "What is the charge?"

"A very serious one," replied the sergeant. "Gun-running!"

"You're raving mad!"

"Do you deny your cargo contained arms?"

"There are a couple of Capchur guns and a supply of darts. They are only used to sedate sick animals."

"Then I shall be interested to hear you repeat that when you are shown the collection of small arms and ammunition which I found in the false bottom of six of those crates which were deposited at my station by this young woman last night. She told me you were bound for Myala which stretches along the border for nearly sixty miles. A convenient place to smuggle supplies across to the rebels."

There was a stupefied silence after that. Jan stood swaying, staring at the wall with blank eyes. Margaret was frightened. He looked so strange it seemed he had travelled to another realm, another time, and this room, the present, had been forgotten. It had all happened so quickly there was no time to collect her thoughts. Had the sergeant gone beserk? Could there really be guns in those crates? The answer was clear. To charge a man with a crime as serious as this he had to be very sure of himself— and Sergeant De Wet had already made one mistake which had sent him to a town like Alwynsrus—yet it seemed incredible that Jan would get involved in a despicable business like this, but Helen's condemnation of the cargoes he flew, plus his determination to make this trip in the Dakota as arranged added up to some damning evidence!

Jan was being dragged across the room when Dr. Gavascar stepped forward. "I have to say that this man is still under my medical care and in my opinion needs complete rest for another twenty-four hours."

"Right," said the sergeant through his teeth, "now you have said it, stand aside . . . unless you wish to sign a statement that you take full responsibility for guarding a prisoner while he is in this miserable place. A *white* prisoner!"

The Indian knew the rules and bowed to the inevitable, but not without a last word. "By taking him from here *you* are assuming full responsibility for his health, I trust."

The sergeant ignored that and ordered his constable to bring Margaret's luggage. "I want you, too," he said. "I'm not sure how deeply you are mixed up in this."

The nurse helped Margaret with the few belongings she had unpacked, and when the constable had taken two of her cases outside, the English girl walked across to Jan's bed to collect his papers in the satchel. He would need them, perhaps.

Now that it was daylight Alwynsrus was seen to be no more than a trading post for a farming community with a general store, miniature bank, petrol pumps and a café as the focal points. The police office looked just as bare when they were marched through to reach the wired compound behind the building. There, the wooden crates stood with their contents spilling around them, and as nobody by then doubted, six of them contained a collection of small guns and ammunition beneath a light layer of sawdust. Jan looked at them with the same stunned resignation he had adopted since leaving the clinic. Not once during the five mile drive had he looked at Margaret; simply stared at the opposite canvas as if it revealed innumerable fantastic pictures. Once, he had lifted his hand to brush away a fly, found he was shackled to the sergeant, and shifted his gaze to the metal ring round his wrist.

The questioning then began. Margaret had to sit outside on a wooden bench watched over by a black constable who stood in the doorway. Two hours passed while the morning grew hotter and hotter. At last, there were sounds of movement within and she was summoned.

"Where is Mr. Schroeder?" she asked, seeing the empty room.

"Safely locked up until I can send him to a city jail. This case is too big for a circuit judge. Now sit down and tell me *your* version of the story."

At the end of the short account of her aquaintance with Jan and how she came to be on the aircraft, Sergeant De Wet stood up with a grunt.

"Umm. He said you were an innocent passenger—that's about all he would say. Why are you concealing a gun?"

"Pardon?" She sounded genuinely surprised.

"One of my men saw you put a revolver into your suitcase last night. He handled it; said it was an expensive weapon."

"Come, come, Sergeant, I realize life must be a little dull around here, but don't let this present excitement run away with you. Surely you have enough guns in those crates without imagining that I have one hidden away." She was using the technique practised by great numbers of English gentlewomen who had frequented the colonies in past years, and that derisory hauteur could still be used to effect, at times. Sergeant De Wet hated them, but was unable to deal with such women. Once, his physical attraction had been enough to make the most toffee-nosed girl change her tune, but these days he seemed to have lost his touch. This *flerric* with the wide green eyes, smooth hair and milky white skin had that aloof tranquillity so many English girls seemed to possess. It made a man long to get her on her knees. Twenty years ago he would have succeeded! Now, he walked across to her suitcases and emptied the contents of them all in a heap on the floor. Margaret burned inside, but kept her calm expression as he pawed through her clothes and personal possessions. Failing to find the gun, he turned his attention to the case at her feet. "What are these?" he asked.

"My surgical instruments. I told you last night that I am a trained vet. Did you think it was a do-it-yourself burglar's kit?"

There it was again: that hauteur which made him feel a fool. He told her to stand up. "There is only one conclusion I can reach," he said with a mean smile, "I shall have to search you."

"There is no need for that. You have already studied me quite closely enough to be sure I couldn't conceal a bulky weapon beneath this dress."

"Not at all. You'd be surprised where people hide them!"

"Then I suggest you ask your wife to perform the task. I saw her briefly last night. That would be the best way out of the predicament, I think."

The game was lost, and he told her she could go. Her request to see Jan was refused and he warned her not to attempt to leave Alwynsrus without telling him. There was not much likelihood of her going anywhere at the moment, she reflected, as she repacked her cases. This town was not exactly a Mecca, an intersection of African highways but, in any case, she would not leave Jan locked away in this isolated spot. Not knowing the legal system operating in this country, it seemed likely that he could wait weeks before his case came up and someone should be here to represent him until Chris could arrive. The authorities were sure to get in touch with him.

When all the clothes were neatly folded into the cases again she realized she had nowhere to go. Rather than ask the sergeant she carried her cases in relays to the general store where she asked the pretty assistant if there was a boarding house near. It seemed the only rooms which might be available were in a small one-storey annexe to the café run by a Greek named Andro-polou. How a Hellene came to be in this part of the world was a mystery to Margaret, but there he was, large as life, when she walked into the pleasant eating-room. It was clean and bright, but hardly well-appointed. Through an open door to the left was a bar which Margaret had already learned she would not be able to enter even had she wanted. Andropolou had a room which she could have for the night until she decided what to do, and he helped her carry in her cases.

The room was only that. Bare walls, bare floor, an old-fashioned bedstead, a wooden chest and an enamel bowl to serve as a wash-basin, but it was *somewhere* and had the advantage of being situated only three doors from the police station. After a rest following lunch, she put on her most comfortable shoes and set off for the clinic. The distance didn't daunt her; at home she walked for miles with the family dogs. For a second, remembrance of her bicycle back in Cape Town brought a wry smile, but it was soon banished because it reminded her of that day at Sea Point when all this had started. Why, oh why, had Jan allowed himself to get mixed-up with such a business? Suddenly Van Heerdon's words at the party took on a meaning. "I know Jan Schroeder. I can buy him any time I like." Was this what he had meant?

Dr. Gavascar was delighted to see her and expressed consternation over what had happened.

"I understand there was nothing you could do," she told him. "Mr. Schroeder and I are very indebted to you for taking us in last night. He might have been very seriously ill if you had not. I have returned to pay you for the treatment we received; there was no chance this morning."

"What will you do now, Miss Ward?"

"I'm not sure. I cannot continue my journey to Myala until Mr. Schroeder's brother turns up."

"Then there were guns in the wooden boxes?"

"I am afraid so." Margaret's eyes appealed to the Indian to comfort her by dismissing the idea of Jan being involved as ridiculous, but he merely wagged his head and told her, "Sergeant De Wet is very powerful in this district. He has invisible eyelids. When his eyes appear to be

104

looking, they are really tightly closed. For this phenomenon many people pay him large sums of money. They are afraid, you see, that the eyelids may lose their power one day. I hope . . ." He tailed off hesitantly.

"Don't worry." She smiled sadly. "I know the dangers of this sort of thing. These people will never stop paying."

Half an hour later she was back on the road, hurrying to reach Alwynsrus before it grew dark. In her handbag was the gun in its webbing belt which she had pushed beneath Jan's mattress that morning as she collected his papers together. She had done it impulsively with no more intention than shielding Jan from a further charge of carrying a weapon. Now, she was maliciously pleased at having put one over on Sergeant De Wet. The thought sustained her until she reached her room. After dinner she went to the police station, hoping to speak to Jan, but her request was again refused. The sergeant was nowhere to be seen and all she got from the black constable was very vigorous shaking of his head and rolling of his eyes.

"When *can* I see him?" she persisted.

The head shaking started all over again and she stormed back to her room. Resorting to tears was not in her nature, but the rich reek of cooking, the bare room, the foreignness of her surroundings, and her complete aloneness brought her very near them that night. What on earth was she to do? The situation was beyond her at the moment, and she sat on her bed, fully-clothed, while she tried to see through the fog of thoughts which clouded her normally sharp brain. In the end, she fell asleep, worn out with worrying, and the lights of the few buildings of Alwynsrus gradually petered out as the inhabitants were deep in slumber, too.

A persistent knocking brought Margaret awake, to find her light still on and the room distinctly chilly. It took her some time to collect her thoughts and recognize the knocking noise. It was coming from her window. Immediate fright made her reach for her bag where she knew the gun would be, but her hand stopped in mid-air when she heard a voice whisper, "Maggie!"

Her heart gave a great glad leap as she ran to open the window. There had been new evidence, and they had released Jan!

4

IT took two seconds, Jan's hand across her mouth and his whispered demand for her to keep quiet to make her realize all was not well. He climbed in through the window and urged her to get her things together.

"Where are we going and what are you doing here?" she demanded in a fierce undertone.

"I broke out of that cell. De Wet is as drunk as a ginned-up rhino and the other two were easy to handle. It was rough on them after bringing us from that aircraft, but I had no option. I'm not sure how long it'll be before they come round. When they do I want to be well away from here."

"You are making things worse for yourself. Surely you are in enough trouble as it is without adding a jail-break to the list," she cried.

"If you don't want to risk your neck by coming, it's all right by me. Stay here and entertain De Wet. From what I've seen and heard, he takes some amusing. Did they take my gun?" He was plainly indifferent to her decision, and as he took the webbing belt from her and strapped it round his waist he said, "Before you tell me killing is a punishable offence I'll explain that I don't mean to shoot anyone. Get a move on, if you want to come."

"I'm ready," she said testily. "As you seem to be 'El Supremo' of this operation, I'm waiting for further instructions."

"Give me two of those cases; you can bring the other one and that case of torture instruments. Now, for God's sake don't make a noise as we go out." He snapped off the light and bent to pick up the luggage. Margaret put out an urgent hand in the darkness to touch his arm.

"Leave my things. You can't possibly carry them in your weak condition. It will be out of the question for you to walk far, as it is."

"We're not walking, sweetheart," he told her softly.

They climbed through the window rather clumsily due to the heavy suitcases, and he led her behind several buildings until they came upon a small canvas-covered truck.

The luggage was thrown in the back and Margaret told to hop in the passenger seat. The engine started with a roar which should have awakened even a sleeping elephant, and Jan swung into the road so suddenly that Margaret was thrown against the door. Driving methods in a car which responded like a dream didn't come off so well in a heavy utility vehicle, but the knowledge didn't deter him in the slightest and they departed from the village like an electric hare at a dog-track. Once clear of habitation, Jan let the lights blaze out and pressed the accelerator. Nothing happened; they were going flat out already. He sighed.

"What I'd give for my Lotus right now instead of this bucket."

Feeling like a character in an animated cartoon, Margaret used his airy unconcern when she asked, "How did you get hold of it?"

"It was there."

She turned to gaze at him. "But that's . . ."

". . . stealing. I know. They really asked for it leaving all the keys in an unlocked box inside the compound."

"You mean . . . oh Jan, you haven't stolen a police truck!"

"Borrowed it."

"They'll catch us before we get any distance."

"What in? I put the other vehicle out of action before I left."

It took her several minutes to recover from that bombshell. The feeling of being part of a cartoon increased. At any moment Jan would start driving up completely vertical mountains and down the other side while the sergeant, in the guise of a fox, would hop about in rage on the opposite side of a ravine. This tall, red-haired man who had seemed merely irresponsible now revealed himself as a calculating opportunist. The suggestion that he was simply putting one over on Chris by flying the Dakota to Myala had been a blind to cover the need to get his cargo of illegal arms to the Game Reserve. He carried a gun and was skilled at breaking free from prison cells—long practice, no doubt! The theft of this truck was commonplace to a man such as he.

"Where are we heading?" she asked faintly, already suspecting the answer.

"Myala."

"To deliver your consignment of arms. I suppose the crates are in the back of this truck?"

There was a short silence, then he said, "That *was* a joke, wasn't it?"

Something about his tone and the way he had suddenly tensed beside her set her heart thumping painfully. "You told me Van Heerdon is a crook, and Helen said you weren't averse to taking doubtful cargoes because he paid you well. Wasn't . . . didn't you really know about the guns?"

He didn't answer and the silence stretched from then until eternity. The truck rushed over the sand road while the two people inside suffered their own anguish of mind. If Jan had played no part in the shipment of guns Margaret had done the unforgivable; hit a man when he was down. Surely, after the ordeal they had been through together she should have been past making comments like that! Her first unfounded accusation could be excused on the grounds that she had had no way of knowing that lightning had forced the Dakota down when everything she had heard had pointed to the likelihood of a fault in the machine. This present false conclusion was unpardonable.

Sergeant De Wet's disclosure had hit Jan between the eyes; she could still visualize the way he had looked. No man could fake such a reaction! So, with a new deep conviction that he was innocent, she tried to fathom why Jan was strengthening the case against him by this impolitic action. With only the slimmest chance of proving he knew nothing of what was in the base of those crates, breaking out from a prison cell and stealing a police truck for his get-away was the very worst thing he could do. There was something in his nature which urged him to paint himself even blacker than he knew people would think him; a sort of defiant "sheep for a lamb" attitude. It was still not clear to her *why* he was scorching along the road to Myala if all the crates were still in the compound at Alwynsrus. It could not simply be to deliver her safe and sound. There must be some other reason burning inside him.

During their short aquaintance she had realized this man was not given to quixotic impulses. There her thoughts pulled up sharply. That was about all she did know about Jan Schroeder. Suddenly she was back at Sea Point that afternoon saying to Helen, "Isn't it time someone tried to understand him!" This was the second time she had had cause to remember her words. She hadn't been working very hard at it. A quick glance showed her Jan was another world away, so she turned her coat collar up against the chill and laid her head on the metal side of the cab where the continual bumping served as a scourge.

Jan had forgotten the girl. The fire inside him had reached white heat and stayed that way, eating into his vitals and making the pain from his leg seem insignificant. This morning, his life, which had been heading steadily downward, accelerated to absolute rock-bottom. The scales had always been weighted against him, the truth had been on the cards plain enough for even a dimwit to see, but he was a fighter by nature and had chosen to struggle against the odds.

However, even the toughest combatant knew when he was beaten. Some time in the future he would pick up the pieces and start again—on his own. Never again would he strive to prove he was capable of impossible qualities, that he could match anything anybody could do, and *never* would he imagine himself able to use a man like Van Heerdon to his own advantage. Sure, he had turned a blind eye to several loads which had exceeded the permitted weight, some others which were not packed in accordance with freight regulations, had twice flown into the bush to pick up a "friend" of Van Heerdon's and asked no questions about his identity or why he couldn't use a normal airline, but none of it was deeply unlawful. Van Heerdon paid double prices for these journeys and he had also put him in touch with several business men who didn't regularly need the services of air freight and were glad to deal with the pilot direct.

All this while Jan had thought he was being smart. He would take a risk or two until he had doubled the profits of Schroeder Freight Limited, then he would drop Van Heerdon like a puff-adder. But he had been caught in his own slipstream. Fury bit into him anew at the recollection of the guns and ammunition which had been hidden beneath the supplies for Russell Martin at the Game Reserve.

Some months ago, Van Heerdon had arranged for Jan to meet a man who could supply packing and crating services considerably cheaper than the firm already used by Schroeder Freight, but Chris had only agreed if he inspected the goods once they were packed. All had seemed square and above-board, so, after four or five months, Chris dropped his scrutiny and even seemed pleased at the cut in costs. Was that when the guns first started being slipped in beneath the legitimate goods?

The Schroeder brothers had been operating from Cape Town for some nine years and were known and trusted by the staff at the airport. On most of their trips it had only been necessary to show the Customs authorities the freight manifest and they had been cleared. Occasionally, one of the men would prise open a crate or two, peer inside, then fasten it down again. It was all done on a friendly basis with plenty of wise-cracking on both sides, especially when the cargo turned out to be a collection of snakes bound for a zoo.

How many times had those laughing men let a consignment of arms pass beneath their noses? How often had he flown to

Myala quite unaware of what was in the freight hold? He had walked right into this situation and deserved the outcome. Whatever else he was, he had always accepted judgement for his actions and cried on no one's shoulder. What he would *not* accept, and what was grinding into him like a dentist's drill was the knowledge that Chris would be automatically drawn into this. Nobody would believe the senior partner of the firm had no idea what was going on. He had taken stuff to Myala himself; he could be implicated right up to his ears!

Jan's relations with his brother had deteriorated very gradually and the more he tried to breach the gap the more intolerant Chris became. The family always backed Chris, of course, so Jan had started finalizing deals *before* telling his brother. They always had a row over it, but Chris usually came round once he got used to the idea. Because of a wife and twins to consider, Chris was inclined to caution, but Jan was not averse to taking a risk here and there if it meant the advancement of the company. Now, he had taken one risk too many and Schroeder Freight would pay the price. Even if their brother George, who was a barrister, could manage to prove Chris was an innocent victim, the good name of the company would be lost. The customers who were already on their books would never trust them again and new customers would steer clear of dealings which involved them.

Chris had lost all he possessed once before, but that had been under almost heroic circumstances. Now, he stood to lose it all again. The downward spiral had started with the purchase of that Dakota. Chris wouldn't listen to his assurances that it was completely airworthy, and when he went behind his back to try to cancel a deal he had given his word on, Jan saw red. Beating him to the post by taking off in the Dakota just as Chris arrived at the airport had been born of his anger, but then Fate had decided to step in with a flash of lightning.

From then on, events had hurtled to the staggering realization that the biggest blow ever to befall the family had been brought about by one of their own number—something none of them would ever forgive. This broken-down truck was not travelling fast enough for his racing pulses. At Myala there was a man who had been waiting to receive those guns, and Jan wanted him! He wouldn't rest until he had sorted out the whole organization, but the man he most wanted to meet again was Elliot van Heerdon!

Thirty miles from Myala the truck ran out of petrol. It was a blessing in disguise because Jan was exhausted, but he cursed and swore at having to abandon it. Margaret jerked awake, and by asking what had happened, broke the awkwardness she had felt without realizing it.

"We'll have to cover the rest on foot," he growled. "Come on, start walking."

"You are in no condition to tramp along these rough roads," she protested. "Have a rest before going on."

"You stay there and wait to be picked up, if you like. Flash your legs at the first driver who comes along and he won't be able to resist you—but don't be surprised if you never reach Myala."

He limped away into the darkness and Margaret sat tight in her seat secure in the knowledge that he wouldn't get very far. Ten minutes later she went in search of him and found him sitting by the side of the road with his head in his hands. Without a word she helped him to his feet and led him, leaning heavily, back to the truck. It didn't take her long to make a bed of sorts with towels and other articles from her suitcases, and as she arranged them on the filthy floor, she reflected that one of her first tasks on arriving at the Game Reserve would be a laundry session.

"Can you swallow aspirin without water?" she asked.

"Yes, if I open this bottle of grog." He indicated a dark bottle just inside the tailboard. "While I was relieving De Wet of the keys, I thought we might get thirsty on the journey. There wasn't time to select the finest vintage from his collection." He pulled the cork and tipped back his head to drink long and thirstily.

"From the smell of that stuff, I'd say the aspirin are unnecessary," she commented dryly, taking the bottle from him. "Lie back before you fall back!" She covered him with several cardigans and settled against the canvas cover. "Before you drift off, what do you want me to do if the police appear?"

"Run like hell," he grunted.

Now they were back in a nurse-patient relationship, Margaret found it easier to say what was weighting her down. Once they arrived at Myala, the chance would be lost and, for some reason, the idea of his flying off to face the outcome of all this with her accusation unrevoked filled her with dismay. Unsure whether he was still awake, she apologized, nevertheless.

"Put my remarks down to hysteria," she began. "You may be used to forced landings, rooms in out-of-the-way Greek hostels, and drunken police sergeants, but my sheltered upbringing in deepest Norfolk didn't prepare me for the harsher side of life. I told you once that fortune had always smiled on me. Perhaps it's time I suffered a little—it might make me more tolerant."

For a while she thought he hadn't heard, then he murmured, "I wish you hadn't said that, Maggie. I now feel honour bound to apologize for not leaving you behind at Cape Town—and who knows where it will end! Before long we will both be in tears. Have a swig from that bottle, then you'll really have something to bash your teetotal conscience with."

She smiled into the darkness. It was all right. He had accepted her words of contrition without feeling she was sorry for him. It was a first faltering step towards understanding this fiery man.

Dawn jumped up like a theatrical back-cloth being rigged. One minute it was night, the next, a panorama of staggering beauty leapt before her weary eyes. To the west, standing sentinel against the lavender sky, was a range of serrated mountains, and before it a great spread of forest looking deceptively green and fertile in the intensity of light slanting from the east. An apricot flush stained the cirrus formations which hung high above, anticipating the arrival of the sun which assaulted this land so fiercely at times.

The stillness, the superlative air of nature uninhibited, filled Margaret with an ache of longing. What for, she couldn't tell, but knew this particular dawn would live for ever in her memory. While Jan slept, free from his torment for a while, she sat as still as a statue, hugging her knees while she acknowledged a strange metamorphosis within herself. She likened the twenty-six years of her life to a cabouchon gem, shining with the peace and serenity of a loving family, a very good education, and a single-minded ambition easily achieved. Now, rather tardily perhaps, Destiny had decided to start adding the facets, cutting ruthlessly into the heart of it and discarding some of the pretty dross so that a jewel of infinitely more value could be produced. There was only one danger. If the cutting edge should make an infinitesimal error when it sliced into the stone, the whole would be ruined and counted worthless.

By eight o'clock the sun was hot enough to make Margaret throw off her coat and look longingly at the bottle at her feet. The need for a drink was too strong, and she picked it up, removed the cork and sniffed. It smelt fairly obnoxious, but she tipped some of the raw brown fluid down her throat experimentally.

"Welcome to the club," said a quiet voice behind her, and she jumped, spilling the liquor down the front of her blouse. "Tut, tut," admonished Jan, "you'll have to learn to carry your drink if you intend taking it up seriously."

She looked at the brown stain spreading across the white material. "That's two nightdresses *and* a blouse you have ruined."

He sat up, pushing off the smothering cardigans. "Don't spread the tale around. People would read highly imaginative meanings into the words." It was said lightly, but she treated it as a serious remark.

"What rubbish! As if we would have time for that sort of thing under these conditions."

"I have never known conditions to be prohibitive." He leant across and pinned her against the canvas with a kiss which proved his point a hundred times over! Taken unawares, Margaret instinctively let herself go limp, and the embrace was over in ten seconds flat. Jan took his hands from her shoulders and slowly looked her over. "My God, woman, you must have fallen into the sterilizer along with your surgical instruments!"

Margaret's face burned red. "There's no need to be insulting because your vanity is hurt. There are plenty of other little girls to play with."

"Yes," he flared, "that's just about your style, isn't it? 'Run away and play like a good lad.' Uppermost in your character, Maggie, is frustrated motherhood—but you have picked the wrong subject. I was separated from the boys years ago."

"And can't resist proving it at every opportunity. You seem to have forgotten you are a runaway jail-bird . . . and a thief," she added for good measure.

"Don't stop there." He was lashing himself now, instead of her. "I bought an aircraft I can't possibly hope to pay for, flew it against big brother's instructions, took you as a passenger and thereby risked your stiff neck, allowed myself to be made a scapegoat by a gun-runner, locked a policeman in his own cell . . ." He stopped, breathing hard. "But don't leave out the super-crime, the daddy of them all. I have put Schroeder Freight on the black list and ruined the family business. For that, I really should stand in the corner with a bloody dunce's cap on my head!"

His anger bit into her like a physical pain. She had never aroused such deep emotion in a person, and didn't like the feeling.

"Please don't," she begged. "I'm terribly sorry."

"I don't want your sympathy," he whipped back. "All I ask is . . . oh, what the hell does it matter!" In a fierce movement he slid to the end of the truck and dropped to the ground. A gasp escaped him as pain from the forgotten leg-wound ran up his thigh, but he lurched away round the vehicle in an attempt to quench his fury, leaving Margaret in as big a turmoil as himself.

He was back almost immediately, staring into her grimy face and liquor-splattered blouse. "There's some sort of building ahead; you can see it from the front of the truck."

"How far is it?" She scrambled to the ground, glad of the diversion, and went beside him to the head of the bonnet. Way in the distance she could make out a break in the thick growth but Jan's *veld*-trained eyes saw more than she did.

"Do you have any money?" he asked.

"Yes. Do you want it?"

"I can't beg for petrol without it." The wounded male lashing out at the female had vanished and Margaret brightened as she fetched her handbag. The prospect of getting mobile would improve the situation no end but, when she realized that he intended walking there, a protest slipped out before she could stop it and she feared he would fly off the handle again. He was sweetly reasonable, however.

"There's no other way. You can't go, however willing you may be."

"Let me come with you."

"And leave all your belongings for any passer-by?" He unstrapped the gun-belt. "Here, this should protect you."

"I couldn't use it if the need should arise," but he had turned and was on his way.

"Jan!"

He half-turned. "Yes?"

"Why do you carry a gun?"

"Self-defence. We get some pretty wild creatures in this country." A twisted smile crossed his lips. "Most men take them when they venture from the cities; it isn't only those with criminal tendencies like me."

He limped away along the road, his hair flaming beneath the sun. He is right, she thought, watching him, the maternal instinct must be very strong in me for the sight of him in those cut-off shorts, filthy shirt, and hardly able to walk in a straight line makes me want to laugh and cry at the same time . . . and oh, I shall be glad to see him come back. Her innate urge for cleanliness set her searching in her cases for a fresh blouse. Then she drenched a handkerchief with cologne to set her face tingling, and brushed her thick dark hair, tying it round with a soft belt from one of her dresses to keep it from her face. The freshness didn't last long.

Within half an hour her blouse was sticking to her and thirst was beginning its torment again. The heat under the canvas cover was already enough to remind her of the ordeal in that aircraft, and she looked longingly at the bottle Jan had brought with him. For ten minutes she fought the impulse, but her will-power seemed strangely weak all of a sudden and she drew the cork and sipped. It was warm and tasted revoltingly sour by now, but it slid over her parched throat with comforting wetness until she could drink no more. A glance at her watch showed her Jan had been away for over forty-five minutes, so she jumped down from the truck to see if she could see him coming.

There was no sign of movement in any direction, which worried her anew. She should have insisted on going with him. Suppose he had collapsed by the roadside! That building was further away than it looked; he would never make it. How long should she wait before going after him? Although the questions were important ones her brain seemed unable to get down to answering them. It was growing unbearably hot, so she pushed up the sleeves of her blouse and undid two buttons to push it away from her neck. The sun was playing tricks with her, making the road jump up and down, and hazing the mountains to a blur. Even the truck seemed out of focus and swung about in a most curious way. She sighed. Where, oh where, was Jan? Since her legs felt rather shaky, she sat down under the trees to puzzle out the problem.

A vehicle approached in a cloud of dust and, as soon as it stopped, Jan got out and limped quickly across to the seated girl. "What is it? Are you all right?" he asked sharply.

A pale face was turned up to him and

the large green eyes held a sad expression. "I thought you had abandoned me!"

"Nothing happened while I was away?"

She shook her head and he continued. "It took a long time to walk there, believe me, but we're in luck. As I thought, that place was part of an Afrikaaner farm and the owner sent me back in a truck with two gallons of petrol. That should get us to Myala. It won't take long to fill up."

He set about doing just that, then handed back the empty cans to the driver, who turned his vehicle round and shot off along the road.

"Nice fellow, that farmer," Jan said conversationally as he screwed on the petrol cap.

Margaret was thinking of Myala and a clinically clean bed in a cool room with blinds drawn against the sun. The picture was so appealing she sank back into the long grass with her eyes closed.

"Steady!" said Jan's voice beside her. "You can't sleep there. You'd better get back in the truck."

She opened her eyes to see him watching her with concern. Yes, concern! "Perhaps it would be wise," she agreed.

He helped her to her feet, noting the movement of her pale breasts through the unbuttoned blouse. It surprised him. There was never any hint of seductiveness about her and he put this lapse down to the assumption that she was now too tired to care. When she swayed slightly as she walked, it seemed to strengthen the idea, but when her knees buckled beneath her and brought a spate of giggles from the girl, a wild suspicion began to hatch in his mind. One glance at the back of the truck was enough. Laughter lit up his eyes and brought youth back to his pain-aged face. He leant against the metal side of the vehicle while mirth got the better of him. Suddenly, optimism struggled to make itself heard through the din of depression, weariness and guilt so that the splendour of his country stirred in his bones and leapt in his blood once more.

"Maggie Ward, you are quite tipsy," he accused joyfully. "I do believe there is hope for you yet."

"I . . . was . . . thirshty," she explained carefully through her paroxysm of tittering.

"I'll say! That bottle is almost empty. You don't start out timorously on the road to ruin, do you?" He had to lift her into the cab, but her limpness pleased rather than angered him this time. Those few seconds with her in his arms brought him a lightning reminder that life still had its brighter side.

They had been several minutes on their way when Margaret said, "Whatever are they going to think when we turn up at Myala like this? You look quite villa . . . villainoush."

"But sober," he said, trying to keep a straight face. "With luck we should be at Russell Martin's place in an hour and a half. The first thing I shall be after is a cigarette. I never thought I could last so long without one."

"You should stop altogether. It only takes will-power."

"Ah . . . but I don't have any."

"Nonsensh," she slurred, "you are the most strong-willed man I have ever met."

"That is only when I want something so badly that I have to fight for it."

"*I* don't have to fight for things," she bragged airily.

"Maybe you have never wanted anything badly enough."

That remark appeared so profound Margaret lapsed into silence and soon the jostling and rocking of the truck sent her to sleep. When she settled against his shoulder Jan sighed. He was fully responsible for putting her through all this. Although the lightning had been no fault of his and normally they would have arrived at Myala quite safely, he had had no right to involve a girl in his scheme to get even with Chris. That she was cool and level-headed in no way minimized his guilt for forcing her to cope with what she had been through. Competent as she was, the experience must have been unnerving for a foreign girl unused to the vast, uninhabited distances of this country. One tended to forget that she might be afraid. It was not that she was one of those hearty masculine females with biceps like a wrestler.

In fact, her curves were firm and exciting, and that freshly-washed, cologne-scented wholesomeness made a man want to bury his nose in her hair and neck while he held her close. No, it was more her assured manner, direct look, and that way of speaking which always sounded slightly aloof and superior to a person who spoke

English prostituted by a national dialect. Then, he hit upon what really roused antagonism in him. She was a goody-goody . . . near perfect . . . which was why he had felt slightly malicious pleasure to find she had been tempted by the only liquid in sight. It would be very satisfying to see her make just *one* mistake before he left her behind at Myala; give just *one* indication that she was as fallible as he. In other words, his masculine arrogance would like to see her taken down a peg or two!

Soon, he came upon the boundary fence of the Game Reserve and followed the track which ran beside it for the best part of an hour. The guard on the gates knew Jan and lifted the barrier while splitting his face with a wide smile. He accepted the arrival of this pilot dressed in filthy clothes and a two-day stubble on his chin, driving a canvas-covered truck with a white woman asleep beside him as if there were nothing odd about the situation. Jan greeted him and was told that Warden Martin was not at the bungalow; had been away for four days or more.

"You go on up, sir, him come back not

very long," said the guard with a roll of his eyes and a boy-scout type salute.

Jan was perturbed as he followed the main track to Russell Martin's bungalow. It was unusual for the Warden to be away when stores were due. If he had set out four days ago he must have meant to be back by Wednesday when Jan should have arrived, and naturally would have made a point of meeting the English girl whom he had invited to work with him. Russell had old-fashioned manners which would not have allowed him to leave her to settle in on her own with only Craig Barker as host. It all seemed highly suspicious now that Jan was aware of the arms being received by someone at Myala, but he shied from concluding that Dr. Martin was involved. Aside from his principles, the man was so completely absorbed in his work he would have no time for an unlawful sideline. Jan jabbed the accelerator. Up ahead lay the answers to several burning questions he wished to ask!

The warden's bungalow was a long, low, wooden building raised from the ground and with a veranda running along two sides of it. It was strictly masculine and utilitarian with no unnecessary trappings, but everything to keep a man content. A vast bookcase held reading matter, ranging from science fiction to a study of diseases in apes; a bar supplied him with pleasing stimulus when the day had gone well and complete oblivion if disaster struck; a record player could soothe him with nostalgia or match his restlessness with wild symphonies. There was a huge refrigerator for supplies, a radio transmitter which linked with the outside world, and a shower alongside wide, airy bedrooms. It was the last two which Jan thought of longingly as he pulled up in front of the steps. Craig Barker appeared on the veranda and leant on the rails, watching Jan trying to alight without wincing.

"Where have you been, man, and what happened to the supplies?" he called. "I got on to Chris, who said you left on Wednesday, as arranged. Now you turn up two days later looking like a tramp. What has been going on?"

Jan raised his hands. "All in good time. First, we want a meal and a shower, then sleep. We are just about done in."

"We?"

"I have Miss Ward with me; the English girl." He controlled a grin. "She is not quite herself at the moment."

The Assistant Warden, a rugged fellow in his mid-twenties, took the steps at a jump and looked in the cab. He whistled through his teeth. "I can't wait to see her when she *is* herself! I'll carry her in."

"You lead the way. I can manage her," said Jan, wishing the open blouse didn't reveal quite so much of Margaret.

"Man, you don't look fit to carry a mongoose much less a cuddlesome *flerric*. Besides, if she is going to be living here, the sooner I get to know her the better." The eager tanned face of the younger man suddenly appeared disturbingly lecherous to Jan, who had no intention of letting Margaret into his clutches.

"Just show me which is to be her room," he insisted, "and I'll take . . ."

"There is no need for either of you to do anything," said a light voice. "I am well able to get myself from A to B without assistance. Have we reached Myala?" This last was addressed to Jan.

"Yes. This is Craig Barker, the Assistant Warden. Doctor Martin is away." He

136

turned to Craig. "Where is he? Do you know? It's not like him to take off when he knew Miss Ward was arriving. Was he aware that we had been delayed?"

The younger man shrugged shoulders. "He went out on Sunday after a sick zebra, and that's the last I saw or heard of him. I didn't start getting concerned until Wednesday, but your failure to turn up replaced one worry with another. I tell you, man, I've had one hell of a week. Chris was raging when I contacted him; said he'd heard from Jo'burg that you'd had to ditch. Then yesterday I had another message from him in Kimberley asking if you had turned up. An aerial search found your aircraft minus stores and people so they concluded you had been rescued. He had some pretty forceful things to say about the welfare of Miss Ward, I can tell you; seems to feel he is responsible for her. Still, that's your worry now. I'll get some boys to unload the stores."

"I haven't got them. All the crates are in the police compound at Alwynsrus."

"Please may I have a shower and a long drink of water?" said the forgotten Margaret in her precise way.

Both men swung round. "Of course," exclaimed Craig. "How thoughtless of us to stand around when you have plainly had a harrowing time. I'll organize a meal while you both clean up. There is only one shower, so you'll have to fight over who goes first. When you feel up to it we'll get things straight, Jan."

Margaret was so long in the shower she had Jan banging on the door demanding entry. In truth, she felt that no amount of washing would make her feel clean, so she stood beneath the glorious spray, soaping her body again and again while she emptied shampoo willy-nilly on her hair. When she had smothered herself in talcum and cologne, slipped into a tangerine sleeveless dress, and combed her damp hair into place, she breathed a blissful sigh. *Now* she was Margaret Ward again, not a scruffy vagabond called Maggie.

They hardly spoke a word during the meal. Craig left them to eat while he worked in his office, and they were both so hungry it was time-wasting to indulge in chat. It had been a sharp surprise to both of them to see the other in a normal state again. Margaret had regained her classic

138

quality and, with it, the suggestion of starched white coats and clinical assessment of emotions. Jan was sorry to see the going of "tipsy Maggie".

His own appearance caused a different reaction in the girl. Newly-shaved and in a clean shirt and shorts borrowed from Craig he no longer evoked a fond, maternal concern in her breast, nor could what she felt be described as "nursy". Covertly her eyes travelled from his hair, darkened to chestnut by the shower, to his freckled face which, now the thick stubble had gone, seemed stronger and more full of character than before. In Cape Town she had seen him either angry or carelessly flirtatious. The events of the past few days had etched themselves on his features, showing more forcefulness than she remembered—or had she not looked below the surface until now? In the aircraft and on the night of his delirium she had seen enough of his body as she tended him, yet now, the sight of his brown throat through the open neck of his shirt and his muscular arms covered with fine golden hairs brought on an oddly breathless feeling. He lifted his eyes and caught her studying him which made her colour rise. Heavens! she thought. Never will I touch alcohol again. It obviously slackens my morals.

They had finished their late breakfast and Jan lit his second cigarette since his arrival as they took a last cup of coffee on to the veranda to join Craig who was anxious to hear their story. No sooner were they seated when a jeep bounced into view through a cloud of dust. The two black Rangers were gesticulating wildly and shouting. Craig stood up and went to see what all the fuss was about, and a heated exchange took place. The Assistant Warden went down the steps in some consternation, and Margaret and Jan walked to the rails as interested spectators. The men brought something from the back of the jeep and laid it on the ground. It was the body of a man, torn and mutilated, with the flies still gathering on it. Margaret gave a cry and flung herself against Jan.

"Good God!" he breathed. "How did an experienced man like Russell Martin get himself savaged by a lion!"

5

AGAINST the advice of both men Margaret refused to go to bed. The horror of what she had seen was better kept at bay with other humans around, but she lay silent on the cane chair while Jan discussed the situation with a rather pale-faced Craig Barker. The body had been found in a quiet place up on some rocks when the Rangers had been on a routine visit to a known lion area. At the moment, the Reserve was closed to visitors, due to an outbreak of disease which was in danger of spreading, and the men had been out looking for affected animals when they climbed on the rocks to look through binoculars.

"The whole thing baffles me," said Jan. "I don't profess to know much about game, but surely lions only attack a man if taken by surprise and threatened. And, having killed his victim, he would devour the body. It is most unlikely that Russell would blunder into a pride by mistake; he once told me he could scent out a lion almost as well as the animal could scent him."

"That's true," agreed Craig, "but the fact remains that his rifle had not been fired so he'd had no time to defend himself. There must be a man-eater out there. It happens occasionally. Once the beast gets the taste of human flesh the desire to kill man is always there."

"Then why wasn't Russell dragged off and consumed?"

Craig shrugged. "Maybe the lion was interrupted."

"Wouldn't he return later?"

"Not necessarily. A lion will kill only as much as he needs. If the interruption was long enough he may have tired of waiting and sought a meal elsewhere."

"That still doesn't explain how the Warden came to be taken unawares in country he knew like the back of his hand," Jan pointed out.

"We shall never know, of course. God, what a way for a man like him to go!" He put his head in his hands. "I suppose I shall have to get on the radio-telephone to the authorities. It's a sad blow for all concerned."

"It's not the only worry you have, man. What I have to tell you will hit you almost as hard as it hit me."

"You are going to be hit even harder when Chris catches up with you," said Craig before Jan could go on. "I'd say you'll go down in round one. My call to enquire what had happened to the supplies touched him on a nerve. Seems you had left in a broken-down aircraft which had seen better days, so the news that you hadn't arrived didn't surprise him."

Jan's lips tightened angrily and Margaret could have hit him for saying, "Yes, we were brought down south of Alwynsrus, right out in the *veld*." He made no mention of the cause of their forced landing, and she daren't. He then went on to tell how Margaret had coped with his gashed leg and the appalling heat inside the aircraft, sparing himself not the slightest bit of blame for all she went through, while the girl found herself getting more and more tense with the effort of not breaking into his narrative to defend him. He would hate her for it! When he reached the part about his early morning arrest Craig's head shot up like a puppet on a jerking string.

143

"Oh yes," affirmed Jan, seeing the incredulity in the other's eyes. "The guns were there . . . and I *didn't* know. Let's get that straight before we go any further."

"Then who . . . ?"

"Exactly! I have a pretty fair idea of who sent them, but it means that someone at Myala is the receiver. Any ideas?"

"No." Craig looked utterly dismayed. "No . . . the Rangers are all known and trusted men."

"But *one* of them is guilty. It may be that he is being forced into it for one reason or another, but it doesn't make the action any less criminal. I have no way of knowing how many times I have been used as a means of transporting their vile consignments, but it's pretty certain this is not the first cargo. Whoever that man is, I want him."

Margaret was beginning to get an inkling of why Jan had made this headstrong bid to reach Myala, and it set fear fluttering inside her. There was no question of his intending to go back to Cape Town to face the music there; he was determined to heap coals on to his implication in this affair. The real reason behind the savage anger which was building up in him was revealed by his next words.

"I shan't rest until I have caught up with every member of the organization. I may have walked into this a willing fool, but I am not going to let Chris be accused of something he has played no part in. If I have to choke it out of them with my bare hands, I'll get them to admit he is innocent."

"I don't see how Chris fits into this," said Craig, bewildered by the other's intensity.

"Are you forgetting that he made two deliveries in October? There's an even chance *he* brought a consignment of guns on each occasion."

"I think you are colouring too vivid a picture," Craig told him. "All this talk of an organization and regular consignments is far too dramatic."

Jan stood up and paced the floor restlessly. "So you think because this is the first time arms have been discovered that it's the only occasion they have been sent? There must be an organization. There are at least four people involved; the supplier, the carrier (me), the receiver here at Myala, and the person across the border to whom he hands the consignment. That is the *minimum* number of people needed for a deal of this nature; there are sure to be many more. You spend so much time up here in the animal kingdom you forget the rest of the world is not as cut and dried." He stopped in front of the Assistant Warden and fixed him with a determined look. "So who unloads and unpacks the stores when they arrive?"

"Now look . . ." Craig began rising in aggressive manner.

"*Someone* has to find out which of your boys is in the pay of these people. Face the facts, man!"

To counteract Jan's determination the younger man said, "There are some factors in all this which don't make sense to me. Before we start accusing my staff there's a lot you haven't explained about your own behaviour. If you were put in the *tronk* what are you doing here? How did the guns get into the crates without your knowledge, and if they were put into the police compound for the night simply for protection, why did the sergeant open them? Are you playing quite straight with me?"

Jan accepted this in his usual manner.

Margaret was beginning to know that slight tilt back of his head and squaring of his shoulders prior to plunging into the absolute truth, however unpalatable.

"That last point is the first one I raised when he took me in—and kept on asking. To my mind, he would only have opened the crates because somebody tipped him off about what he could expect to find. If that were so, it would mean I had been deliberately framed . . . which didn't make sense whichever way I looked at it. At first, he refused to answer my question, and we reached a stalemate. I made it plain I wouldn't talk until he did, so after a lot of side-stepping and wandering around the point, he passed it off with the excuse that it was necessary to get details of the contents in order to complete the paper work. Maggie couldn't provide the information, and the cargo manifest was with my other papers at the clinic. I knew it was a fabricated excuse, but it told me I hadn't been betrayed by an informer."

He sat down again at this point and leaned his elbows on his knees, gazing out across the thorn bush which was a feature of Myala. "Man, was that police sergeant a *skurk*! It didn't take long for me to catch on to his activities out there in that tiny place, and I realized he had opened the crates with a view to helping himself to anything which might be of use to him. What he did find was as staggering as gold in the Kalahari. To a man who had been appointed to Alwynsrus to finish his police service in obscure monotony, a discovery of this nature should have been the chance of a lifetime. The uncovering of a gun-running operation would surely boost his worth a hundred-fold, but he is past the stage of wanting to recoup his good standing among his fellow-men. For too long he has been corrupted by his desire to thumb his nose at those responsible for putting him where he is, and once he stopped to think saw only the opportunity to turn his stroke of luck into hard cash.

"As the day wore on he paid frequent visits to the outer building which served as a cell, and his approach changed each time I saw him. When he had no success in drawing any information from me regarding the arms organization, he began to believe that I was an innocent victim and put out ill-disguised offers of how much it would cost me for him to accidentally leave the key in the door of the cell." Jan gave a short laugh. "Ironically, I was turning into an embarrassment for him. He had no desire to turn me in for the mere congratulations he would receive from his superiors; there was more reward in selling me my freedom and disposing of the arms himself."

"So how much did you pay him?" asked Craig woodenly.

Jan ignored that. "De Wet was pretty sure I would keep quiet about his holding on to my cargo; I would only incriminate myself along with him. On the surface, I thought he was on to a good thing—I did desperately want to get out of that cell— but his keyed-up nervousness found an outlet in drink, and that was his downfall. I played him along until well into the night when he was completely stupefied. After that, it was easy."

Craig looked furious. "You damned fool! We shall have the police along here after you."

Jan shook his head. "I don't think so. That sergeant will cut his losses and content himself with what he can get for the contents of the crates. Can you see him reporting the escape of a possible gun-runner while he was too drunk to stand— and in a police vehicle, at that!"

"You mean that truck . . . ?"

"It was the only one available. Don't worry, I'll drive it out of Myala when I leave tomorrow."

The young Assistant Warden walked to the rail and leant heavily on it while he absorbed the incredible facts Jan had presented him with. At last, he turned to lean back against the wooden hand-rail.

"I'd be obliged if you'd leave now." He held up a defensive hand. "Yes, yes, I quite appreciate what a mess you have landed yourself in and I sympathize, I really do, but I have to think of the situation here. With Russell dead, there's a lot at stake. Someone will have to take over as Warden and if I play my cards right there's no reason why they need look further than me. I can't afford to have the authorities hearing of some vague suspicion of gun-running at Myala. You have always been a bit wild, Jan, but simply because your dubious activities have mushroomed into something bigger than you bargained for, I cannot allow you to start harassing my staff and nosing around these premises. In the long run, I think it would be wiser to cancel the contract to fly-in our supplies and that should solve the problem."

He had hardly said the words when he found himself flat on his back on the wooden veranda. Margaret sat up aghast as Jan stood over him, breathing hard.

"Stand up, you bastard, and I'll do it again! Russell Martin is not yet in his grave and you are bloody well placing yourself in his shoes. Chris signed that contract with Russell when you and I were still in school and this is the first time Schroeder Freight has failed to deliver as arranged. The company will supply replacement stores within a week—there is a clause which covers non-delivery due to an accident—and the contract will run to its expiry date. If the new Warden (whoever he may be) decides not to renew we'll accept his decision, but a jumped-up jackal like you has no authority to discontinue an honourable business agreement for no other reason than his own bloody ambitions!"

Craig sat up, wiping away the trickle of blood from his cut lip with the back of his hand. He had forgotten what a tornado this man could be on the subject of his brother, or anything connected with him. Jan still had the light of battle in his eye when he continued, "And before you get on your feet, we'll straighten out another matter. Since the guns were put in the crates at Cape Town and I was making no stops on the way, there can only be one destination for them. I'll leave just as soon as I know which of your boys was hoping to pass them over the border. I can do it with or without your help, but I promise you'll find it easier to agree. You seem to have forgotten that someone in this reserve is making money by aiding the slaughter of human lives, but by God, if necessary, I'll drive the facts home to you in a way you won't easily forget."

Margaret watched with growing dismay. From a comradely discussion between two contemporaries, it had developed into a bitter clash of personalities. Jan's assault on Craig had frightened her. Here, with a vengeance, was evidence of the Schroeders closing ranks. While he met any attack on himself with that familiar stone-wall acceptance, let anyone dare malign or double-deal one of the family and he became a savage defender lashing out at the antagonist. Indeed, it seemed he fully intended taking on all-comers in his effort to clear Chris of any involvement in the gun-running, and Margaret had no doubt he would fight to the bitter end.

It was hard to believe here was the same man she had seen surrounded by jet-setters at Van Heerdon's party. She recalled her own conviction that that sort of life was not really his scene. But for a flash of lightning she might never have had the proof of her conviction, and she certainly would have remained in ignorance of Jan's deep personality. The past two days in his company had shed a very faint light on the complexity within him and she longed to know more. There was so much of him which was yet unprobed—and would remain so, she thought gloomily. It didn't occur to her that she was thinking of him in terms of an interesting species to be studied under a microscope. Although he had had ample opportunity during their long drive, Jan had made no attempt to tell her of De Wet's offer to sell him his freedom, or his own plan to hunt down the men who had used him to carry their illegal cargo. Ah, but of course, she had condemned him before he spoke a word!

Looking at him as he maintained his belligerent stance over Craig who was staggering to his feet, she realized he was not even aware of her presence; that his entire being burned only with the desire to get his revenge. He had brought her to Myala simply because Schroeder Freight had undertaken to get her there, not from any personal liking or chivalrous instinct. As far as he was concerned, she had been delivered and could now be forgotten.

By the time the sun was high in the sky, Margaret had surrendered to tiredness and gone to her room. It seemed the only thing to do. The men set about the task of investigation, first in the store-room, then when that proved fruitless, set off in a jeep to visit a Ranger post somewhere deep in the sheltering bush. Neither of them had taken any notice of the girl sitting so quietly and seemed to have forgotten her very existence when they ran down the steps to the waiting vehicle. They both wore grim expressions and she noticed each had a gun belt strapped round his waist. It worried her. In their present mood anything could happen! Not only that, with a leg which was plainly still giving him a lot of pain and a lack of sleep which would be of no help to his tense state, Jan was not fit to go bumping over rough tracks in a temperature which stood well in the eighties.

Her deep, exhausted sleep was broken by a knocking on her door. It was the houseboy-cum-cook, who was in a panic because Mr. Schroeder was on the radio-telephone demanding to speak to her. He was angry and didn't wish to be kept waiting! She pulled on a cotton housecoat and followed the boy along to the office where he explained the simple two-way system.

"Hallo, Jan," she ventured experimentally.

"It's Chris," said a virile voice so like Jan's it seemed incredible it could not be his.

"Oh . . . Chris!" Relief, disappointment, and embarrassment all intermingled in those two words.

"Are you all right, Margaret? What the blazes is going on up there? Where is Jan?

The boy says you are the only person there. Where are all the others?"

"Please don't ask so many questions at once. I have only just woken up," she said as she played for time. What on earth was she to tell him?

"Sorry," he said on a softer note, "but I have been extremely anxious since you left on Wednesday."

"Yes, I realize you must have been, but there is no cause for alarm." She crossed her fingers as she said that. "I feel as right as rain . . . and Jan has been wonderful," she added hurriedly, seeing an opportunity to get in a little propaganda. "We were struck by lightning and he made a difficult landing in a storm. What a fantastic pilot he is!"

"Er . . . yes. Lightning, did you say?"

"I have never seen such flashes. And when the engine burst into flames it was a sight I shall never forget. I was terrified, but Jan remained quite unperturbed and I put my complete faith in him."

"Mmm. Were you sitting beside him, then?"

"Oh no," she assured him. "He wouldn't

156

let me anywhere near the controls. He was most insistent on that!"

There was a short pause, then: "Nice try, Margaret, but you couldn't have seen anything unless you were in the co-pilot's seat. He won't thank you for trying to cover up for him." When she didn't speak he went on: "Now, just what are you doing at the bungalow alone? Where are Russell, Craig and my brother?"

"There has been an accident. Doctor Martin is dead."

"Dead!" His voice betrayed that he was badly shaken. "How did it happen?"

"It appears he went off four days ago and didn't return. Two Rangers brought in his body this morning—mauled by a lion."

"*What!*" shouted Chris. "Never! Russell Martin knew more about animals than anyone in the Republic. It's inconceivable that he would die in that manner."

Margaret was bewildered. "We saw him . . . Jan saw him, and had no doubts."

"Well, I have! Nobody will convince me a man like Russell would end his life at the mercy of a lion. He must have had a heart attack . . . something like that. I'll concede his body may have been mutilated by some animal *after* death. There'll be a post mortem, of course. Craig Barker hasn't accepted Jan's theory?"

"I . . . I don't know what he thinks. We had only just arrived when they brought in the body. It was a nasty shock, Chris, and everyone is a bit jumpy now."

"Yes, of course. I'm sorry, Margaret. I had known Russell for over fifteen years, ever since he took over Myala, and I had a great respect for him. I suppose you are alone because Craig and Jan are out looking for evidence."

"Yes," she said, thankful for the lie he put into her mouth. There was such a long pause, Margaret thought he had gone.

"Of course, this makes things very awkward for you. I suppose you haven't had time to sort out what you intend doing?"

His words took her off guard. Events had chased one another so fast since her arrival at Myala it had not struck her yet that her own plans had suffered a severe set-back. Would the new Warden be willing to have her here? If Craig should get the post, she had grave misgivings about their relationship remembering his eagerness to carry her from the truck that morning. It was one thing to work cheek by jowl with a man of fifty-two who thought of nothing but animals; quite another to be the constant companion of a lusty twenty-six-year old when there is no other woman for miles around. Certainly it would be impossible to stay there alone with him until a man arrived to replace Dr. Martin.

"Margaret, are you still there?"

"Yes," she said.

"Margaret! Margaret Ward, are you there?"

She realized she hadn't switched the transmitting button and hurriedly did so. "Sorry, Chris, I wasn't thinking."

"Normally I'd leave Jan to return on an inter-city flight, but under the circumstances, I think I'll come up to Myala in the Trilander in the morning. You can return with us, if you wish."

"Oh no!" The frantic protest was out, and she tried to dilute it by saying, "Please don't worry about me. I'm sure you have other commitments."

"Not at all. I feel very responsible for you after all Jan has put you through. If he had let me fly you up there, as arranged, this would never have happened. I am only thankful you are both unhurt. Is it too much to hope the supplies escaped damage?"

That stumped her, so she didn't answer. "Margaret?" said Chris sharply and on impulse she replied: "Chris, are you still there? I can't hear a thing."

Thirty seconds later after ignoring his urgent messages and repeating her avowal that she couldn't hear him, she gently switched off the machine and returned to her room all churned up inside. Curse Jan! The wretched man now had her lying on his behalf—why, she couldn't say—but some instinct told her if Chris arrived up here to interfere in this affair it would be Jan's complete downfall. He *had* to be allowed to cope with it alone.

The men returned shortly after seven when dusk was settling over the long grass and strange trees which hid the wild beautiful creatures of Africa. Margaret had been sitting on the veranda watching and listening as the day of man drew to a close and that of the animal quickened into a battle of instinct and guile, attack and defence. For the first time since her arrival, excitement leapt inside her at the thought that, out there, not many hundred yards distant, were lions, elephants, rhinos and endless varieties of animals which were less universally known, but which possessed a charm and fascination for any ecologist.

Already, the vast distance was tuning-up vocally and her blood pounded with the unfamiliar savagery of it. The going of the sun had endowed the landscape with shadows and nuances which might, in some people, induce unease and a dislike of being alone, but Margaret found it cast a spell over her and she strained her eyes in the half-light to keep the image before her as long as possible. If things had happened according to plan she might have been relaxing here with Craig and Dr. Martin while they discussed their work . . . and Jan Schroeder would have walked out of her life the same day he had hurtled in. She wished desperately that it had been so. Since encountering Dr. Eggerton at that party at home her plans to travel half across the world to Myala had gone smoothly, until an orange car had shot into a driveway and sent her flying. Since then, Jan had wrought havoc in her life while remaining completely indifferent and uncaring of the fact. Helen had been right to say the odds were against Margaret. Instead of *her* taming the lion, *he* had begun to make her equally wild!

The arrival of the jeep brought the return of another problem. What was she to do about her conversation with Chris? Deeming it wise to tell Jan at least part of it—the houseboy was sure to inform the men Chris had called—she decided not to mention the probability of Chris's arrival tomorrow. Jan had enough to cope with for tonight. The moment was delayed by the men wanting a shower and a meal after their heavy day, and over dinner they were a silent group. The breach between the men had not been repaired by the hours spent in the bush; the violent confrontation had not been forgotten—probably never would be. Their manner told Margaret they had had no success in their search and she wondered what the next step would be. Jan looked physically and emotionally drained. Unless he got some sleep he would knock himself up completely and be unable even to face that meeting with Chris which she dreaded.

Over coffee she broke into the half-hour silence by saying, "That leg of yours needs a new dressing, Jan. Come along to the laboratory in a minute and I'll fix it."

He dragged his eyes from the distant visions they pursued. "Right," he said economically.

This diversion provided Craig with the opening he needed and he stood up. "I'll say good night. No doubt you both wish to turn in early, and I have some paper work to do." He paused in the doorway, cup in hand. "I'll get on to the authorities about Russell. Can't leave a body too long in this climate." He raised a hand and was gone.

Jan was anxious to get the medical treatment over quickly and the minute Margaret finished her coffee they walked along to the laboratory she had inspected earlier in the day. It was beautifully equipped, and she stifled a sigh on entering. It would have been exciting to work here with a man like Dr. Martin, but there seemed no alternative but to return to Cape Town with Chris until the situation at Myala was resolved. Maybe it would be possible to take up residence here at a later date. Disappointment stabbed her again. This was the first set-back in her career; it had progressed so smoothly until today. Too smoothly? suggested an inner voice. Isn't it time you suffered a few reverses to shake your complacence? The inner voice was soon drowned by her natural one saying, "Sit up on that bench, will you? It won't take a minute."

When he had been stretched on the floor of the Dakota, it had seemed quite impersonal; now, handling the thigh of a man smouldering with anger, and in a position which necessitated standing a bare foot or so away from him, became an embarrassment. To cover it she adopted her best "nursy" tones as she admonished him for overdoing things.

"You are putting an impossible strain on these stitches, Jan. Dr. Gavascar did a good job, but it was a wide gash and no matter how tough you think you are, your flesh will only stand so much before it tears again. You *must* rest!"

"All right, all right, don't embark on a lecture, Maggie. I'm going to bed as soon as you have finished. I don't think I can take much more; the whole place is swimming around me."

She looked up with exasperation. "Did you wind your mother round your little finger when you were young?"

"Eh?"

"You have the knack of dragging sympathy from a woman when she is at her most annoyed with you."

"Have I? Your frustrated mothering instinct coming to the fore again?"

Oh, she had walked right into that one! It would be better to concentrate on swabbing the puckered flesh slashed by black sutures and keep a still tongue in her head.

"I don't think I held that much sway over my mother," he said. "With seven children to cope with she was kept pretty busy and I, being the youngest, always had one of the older ones keeping an eye on me."

"I have one sister, that's all. What's it like being one of a large family?" She kept her head bent over her task.

"Hectic."

"Are your brothers like you?"

"Not a bit," was the quick reply. "Randell, the eldest, is an eminently respectable director of a wine importing firm—his own. George is a barrister—very upright, honest and law-abiding." He stopped there and she looked up.

"You and Chris I have met. Who is the other one?"

"Kip . . . Chris's spiritual twin."

"Is he a business man?"

"He owns Doringdraai; a farm he bought and developed practically single-handed. The family all said he'd never be able to make a going concern of the broken-down place, but he did—of course."

"Why 'of course'?" she asked immediately.

"Because he is Kip. And is your sister like you . . . cool, competent and damned inquisitive?"

She countered that with, "I spoke to Chris on the radio this afternoon," then wished she hadn't. "Don't look like that . . . I didn't tell him anything."

"You must have said *something*."

"I had to explain about Doctor Martin since he would be bound to hear about it. Luckily, he assumed you and Craig were out hunting for clues and I didn't disillusion him. Apart from that, we discussed how I was feeling, how lucky it was that we both escaped unhurt from the aircraft, what I planned to do now, and . . ."

"Oh, good lord above!" exclaimed Jan with dawning realization. "Russell's death puts you in a hell of a spot, doesn't it?"

"Yes. Since it was by personal invitation from Doctor Martin that I came, I feel I can hardly stay here after what has happened."

"Of course you can't stay. You'd be raped by young Craig at the first opportunity. Oh, I don't know," he amended thoughtfully, "perhaps you wouldn't."

The tensions of the past few days suddenly found relief in her laughter. The ludicrousness of his pondering the controversial loss of her virginity in the midst of the disaster surrounding them kept her laughing merrily with the bandage half-wound round his leg. He watched her with pleasure, and had to thrust back the stirrings of desire. By the overhead light, the sheen of her hair lay darkly against creamy skin, and her eyes held beckoning emerald lights which had not been apparent before. The lips curved in amusement were soft and moist. Most fatal of all was the sharp, clean scent of cologne which, to an exhausted and dispirited man, brought an overwhelming desire to gather her close and seek sweet solace.

Her amusement tailed off when he said brusquely, "I can finish this myself. Go on off to bed!"

"I have to clear up first," she mumbled.

"I'm capable of throwing away a couple of swabs and a bandage wrapper. It doesn't take a veterinary degree to do that!"

She dropped what she was doing and walked to the door. "Good night, then."

"Good night," he said. "And Maggie . . . thanks for not telling Chris."

She smiled bleakly. "All part of my general competence!"

After four hours of dream-troubled sleep Margaret was awoken by noises outside. Fitful moonlight was drenching her room and she glanced at her travelling clock. One a.m. Surely Craig wasn't still working! The beginnings of a headache sent her across the room to her handbag for aspirin, and a glance along the veranda showed her there was no light in any other room. For a brief moment she remembered Craig saying that, once a lion had tasted human flesh he became an addict, but dismissed the notion of the king of beasts prowling round the bungalow as fanciful nonsense.

She returned to her bed and reversed her pillows in the hope of finding a cool surface for her throbbing head. As was usually the case, once her sleep was broken it took her a long time to settle again and the bitter disappointment of having to leave Myala so soon after arriving lay as heavily on her as heartburn. Destiny was cutting into the gem of her life with a vengeance since she had been in Africa. Perhaps there was something about this country which made it impossible for those in it to lead peaceful, uneventful lives. Maybe the wild grandeur of its landscape and animal life reflected itself in the human habitants. Was there any other country in the world which contained such a mixture of pride and prejudice, conflict and endeavour, truth and misunderstanding? Jan, perhaps, typified the land of his birth; restless, stubborn, idealistic, always striving—but intensely loyal to what he believed in. Would she have to return to England to find contentment?

There, suddenly, was the sound of movement once more, and it could not have been a killer-lion using such a light, stealthy tread. Knowing she would remain apprehensive until she found the cause, Margaret slipped her feet into mules beside the bed and crossed to the door by the light of the moon. Every room was still in darkness and not a sound could be heard apart from the cries and squeals which were part of the nocturnal hunting pattern in a Game Reserve. She shivered in the warm night. Death stalked out there for the weak and timorous!

Next minute, she detected a faint movement as a board groaned further along the veranda and she instinctively drew back into her doorway. A man walked down the steps and into the shadowed area beyond the bungalow where he spoke in low tones to a companion. From the way he had descended Margaret thought he had been carrying something heavy. If the meeting was harmless why was it necessary to conduct it in the darkness, and so furtively? The ensuing silence suggested they had moved away and she lost no time in flitting along to Jan's room with every intention of waking him.

It was an almost impossible task for he

slept heavily and completely, and no amount of shaking had any effect on him. After repeated pokings and proddings from Margaret, he eventually rolled over towards her and fought his way up into half-wakefulness. She bent to his ear.

"Jan . . . wake up, it's important!"

For the following fifteen seconds it was like battling with an octopus. In his semi-comatose state, his hands had felt her smooth softness, and the rest came naturally. Just as she was wondering how it would all end he seemed to get the message and surfaced completely.

"Oh . . . it's you!"

"At last!" she breathed, recovering from the wrestling match. "When you knocked at the window of my room at the Greek restaurant I obliged by opening my eyes immediately. What does it take to wake you up?"

"An unwilling woman," he grumbled softly. "I know why you *didn't* come, now tell me why you did."

Her news had a quicker effect on him than she imagined it would. He was out of bed and into a pair of shorts before she had time to register that he really did sleep as nature made him. "Stay there!" he commanded her in an undertone, and vanished swiftly.

He was gone so long she had curled up on the bed leaning back against his pillows when he slid quietly into the room.

"Well?" she asked. "Who was it?"

"I don't know. There was no one in the immediate vicinity and, from what I could see, every man is in his bed."

"I'm positive I saw someone."

"I believe you. Beyond the Rangers' quarters is a jeep loaded ready for a journey. The man I want is planning to slip away from here at first light. When he does I want to be ready." He began pulling on a shirt and buttoned it while he looked around him. "It was here on the table, I swear it was!"

"What was?"

"My gun. The bastard must have been in and taken it. Hell and damnation! That puts me at a disadvantage right away."

"Jan, are you sure you know what you are doing?"

"Quite sure," he said firmly. "Go back to your room and rest."

"How can I!"

"By making a real effort." He turned her round and pushed her towards the door. "Lock your room and I'll tell you all about it in the morning."

"Where will you be?"

"Watching over that jeep. Now, get going!"

It was one of the most anxious nights she had experienced. Inactivity at times of tension is the hardest thing to bear, and Margaret tried everything she knew to still her nerves while she waited for the dawn. The hours snailed past as she recited to herself all the symptoms of foot and mouth disease, distemper, and various swine fevers. Then she mentally conducted a Caesarean birth on a mare, spayed a bitch, and removed a cancerous growth from a cat. All this kept her mind off Jan sitting out there in the darkness, but so exhausted her that she fell asleep fifty minutes before the first lightening of the various shades of dawn.

The roaring engine deceived her into a memory of an orange Lotus, but the reality of lying in bed pushed her eyelids up in a panic. That was no luxury car, it was a jeep, and the sound was fading away in the distance. It was barely any lighter than before as she stumbled down the steps and looked wildly around. Where were the Rangers' quarters? The faint sound of voices from the right gave her her answer, and she ran in that direction. Huts loomed up as blacker shapes and the voices grew louder. Her eyes had grown accustomed to the swiftly paling light by the time she turned the corner and saw a group of excited Africans gathered round something on the ground. A quick flash-back to the travesty of a man who had once been Russell Martin brought bile rising in her throat, but she *had* to see what was causing their consternation. As one by one they became aware of the white woman in a brief cotton gown, they fell back with the words dying on their lips until all that could be heard were the agonized gasps of the man lying in the dust, bent double.

"Don't stand there, help him!" she cried, and went on her knees to see how badly hurt he was. "Jan, what have they done to you? Is it safe to move you?" She sounded calmly professional despite her inner fears. He would accuse her of being "nursy" again.

He couldn't answer. Every indrawn breath turned into a spasm of coughing and retching, and his knees were drawn up in pain. A swift examination told her he was not wounded in any way; there was no blood except on his mouth and the side of his head where the small gash had been re-opened. The Africans, recognizing authority and competence, followed her instructions to help the hurt man back to his room, but seemed reluctant to tell Margaret what had happened . . . if any of them had, indeed, seen it . . . then vanished to their own quarters.

For a good ten minutes Jan lay on the bed, fighting to gain control of his breathing while Margaret looked on, knowing she could do nothing to help him. When he made an effort to sit up she told him to stay where he was for a little longer.

"You told me you knew what you were doing," she accused.

"So I was wrong," he croaked. "I wasn't expecting him to have two companions. They held me while he had a field day. I suspect he lost his temper and took his revenge for being made to look a fool in front of you this morning."

"You mean it was Craig?"

"Yes. Surely you realized that!"

6

AFTER giving him a drink of water Margaret tried to wipe away the blood from his mouth, but he pushed her aside and dashed the back of his hand across the oozing cut.

"Don't fuss! You'll be wanting to kiss it better in a minute. I don't have time to be mothered. The longer I wait, the worse it will be. I have to get after them." He started to get off the bed, but staggered and sat down again.

Margaret seized her chance. "Whether you like it or not you are going nowhere for at least an hour." She pushed him flat on his back. "Therefore you have no choice but to be mothered. While you tell me about Craig I'll clean up your face . . . not that it will improve that scowling expression. Then, I'll get you some breakfast."

"I'll give you ten minutes to act nurse, after that I'm off," he vowed, "so make the most of it."

"Please explain about Craig," she said, returning with the sticking plaster, cotton wool, small bowl of water and scissors.

"Russell Martin's death scared him badly—that much must have been obvious even to you. Once I had a good look at the body I realized he had been murdered. I couldn't accept that a lion had attacked him."

"Chris thought the same. He said he wouldn't believe it even if you did." She cursed herself for that slip.

"Yes, that's Chris, all right," he mumbled through the cotton wool.

"It's my fault for telling him you had no doubts. Why didn't you voice your real opinion?"

"Because Craig went along with my first hasty analysis and I began to get suspicious. If *I* could see those injuries were faked to look like an animal attack *he* must surely have reached the same conclusion . . . but he continued to expand the theme with a lot of nonsense about killer lions which may have fooled you but increased my conviction that he was not playing straight. His sudden desire to get rid of me was a little too dramatic, and although he has always

178

been ambitious, he has more sense than to think the authorities would promote him as Warden at the age of twenty-six."

"Are you telling me that Craig murdered Dr. Martin?" Margaret halted with the iodine half-way to his face.

"No, I would hazard a guess that his pals across the border were responsible for that. Aaah! Watch what you are doing with that stuff!" he cried as she dabbed his cut lip.

"Sorry. Shall I kiss it better?"

"You wouldn't know how!" He sat up slowly and shook his head to clear the giddiness. "Your ten minutes are up. If I wait any longer their dust will settle."

Margaret watched with some misgivings as he rose painfully to his feet, and asked, "What are you hoping to gain? There are three of them against one, they are armed and you are not . . . and I fail to see how this recklessness will help Chris, or Schroeder Freight. That *is* why you are being so pig-headed, isn't it?"

He ignored her and went through to the veranda, but she followed him. "Jan, if you kill them you'll make matters a hundred times worse."

He turned to face her. "What the hell do

you take me for! Go back to your test tubes, you are beginning to sound almost emotional."

She showered and dressed quickly, keeping an eye on Jan as he filled the stolen police truck with petrol and swung a couple of cans in the back as spares. Then he collected several water bottles to hang from a hook in the driving cab, and stowed away a container which probably contained food. Margaret ate an apple while she boiled a kettle for two mugs of instant coffee, and when it was ready, took one out to him.

"Oh, thanks," he said, turning from his task and taking the coffee. "What are you all dressed up for?"

She was in a cream skirt and blouse, with a wide cotton hat on her head and a shoulder-bag slung over one arm. "I'm coming with you."

He nearly scalded himself. "Don't be bloody ridiculous! You have been dragging on my conscience long enough. I've delivered you safely to Myala—now stay here."

"I can't. I'd be terrified to stay in this place with a handful of Africans. Please, Jan, you can't go off and desert me. I don't know a thing about this country and its people."

"You'll be all right," he assured her roughly. "I've never seen you unable to cope."

"Of course not . . . because *you* have always been with me. If you go away I'll have no one to turn to, and when it grows dark I shall imagine horrors in every shadow."

For the first time in their relationship she reverted to feminine guile. Contrary to his belief, she knew how to use the weapons with which nature had endowed her, and turned upon him the full battery of wide, frightened eyes, pleading frailty, and subtle flattery of his male superiority. He was a man . . . and fell for it, of course. The memory of her bending over him in a brief cotton gown with her hair tousled round her face made him sigh and rub at the back of his head with an agitated hand.

"I . . . oh, damn it, I'll have to get a message to the authorities and tell them to send someone to collect you. I'll go across and instruct one of the Rangers to get through on the radio as soon as he can. Don't worry, they'll rescue you before nightfall." He drained the mug and limped off towards the huts where he had been beaten up that morning.

The Africans were all there. Now the white Wardens had gone they were unwilling to do anything decisive. With the instinct of the true African they sensed there was trouble ahead and stayed in their quarters, unwilling to become involved. Most of them were aware that Russell Martin had been murdered—the method was not unknown to them—and feared being drawn beneath the wrath of the killers. Tribal warfare was still rife, and they knew the penalties of falling foul of certain factions.

When Jan returned he found Margaret sitting in the passenger seat of the truck, bag and dark glasses in her lap, looking all set to go with him.

"What's the idea?" he asked sharply.

"You do intend leaving now, don't you?" It was sweetly enough said.

"Yes . . . alone. I've fixed for a message to be passed on your behalf. He'll get through at nine o'clock."

"I'm not stopping here without you, Jan. You promised you wouldn't leave me."

This time she must have overdone the performance because he saw right through it and cursed himself for having been such a fool.

"Oh, no, you don't, Maggie. You may have looked pathetically innocent in that baby outfit you sleep in, but the 'poor little me' act doesn't fit the girl you have reverted to. Get out and stop being a damned nuisance. I have wasted enough valuable time over you as it is. Stay here and use that female ploy on whoever turns up to rescue you."

"You are not fit to go off alone."

"OUT!" he insisted.

"No."

"Now look here . . ."

"Where would you have been without me in the Dakota!"

"If you are not out in ten seconds, by God, I'll drag you out," he said through gritted teeth. "This is no time to start playing sex games."

In answer to that she reached across and switched on the ignition.

"Right!" he stormed, losing his patience and his temper. "You bloody well asked for it."

Their departure from the headquarters would not have disgraced Le Mans, and Margaret received the beating Jan would love to have given her from the hard seat as she was literally bounced up and down like a ball. He took a vicious pleasure in hitting all the ruts as he drove flat-out along the rough track, and hoped most heartily that his unwelcome passenger would be black and blue with an elephantine headache before long. At a time like this he could not bother with her idiotic attempts at being provocative. Many a girl had found herself regretting having pushed him too far and ended up being forced to carry out what she had threatened. He had done, on Margaret's behalf, all that could be expected of him. If she was determined to put herself through further discomfort it was her affair. He no longer felt responsible for her, and certainly was not going to waste valuable time by arguing and attempting to pull a struggling female from a seat she was determined to occupy.

When he eventually abandoned the truck she could drive herself back to the bungalow. A fresh surge of anger heated him when he thought of the time he had lost by falling for that show she had put on. How in heaven's name had he been so easily taken in when the performance had been more worthy of one of his girl-friends than this smooth Englishwoman! Every lurch set his own head throbbing and did nothing to aid the gnawing ache low in his stomach, but he kept going as a reminder to himself never to underestimate her again.

Margaret was not at all sure why she had let herself in for this punishment. The maternal instinct seemed to be growing alarmingly, for she had been unable to accept the idea of Jan dashing off into the wilds with no one beside him although it was a sure bet he would be dead against her accompanying him. She had thought she had him over a barrel until he foiled her with the solution of using the radio-telephone. There had been no alternative but to start being precocious . . . and now he was so mad she dared not speak to him.

Every so often she scanned the golden sky for any sign of an aircraft. If Jan found out that she knew Chris was flying in to Myala this morning a wrung neck was the very least she could expect—from *both* the Schroeder brothers! Chris was assuming she would have told Jan of his proposed arrival, and what *his* reaction would be when the Africans informed him his brother had driven off was better not to dwell on. Although she had got her way, it was at considerable risk to tempers and opinions. Maybe she had mishandled the situation, she thought with a downward plunge of her spirits. I am not equipped to cope with life lived at this level and it seems to be controlling *me* instead of the other way round.

A sudden picture flashed before her dust-filled eyes of her sister Alison rushing home from work so that she could go to a pre-Christmas party with young Mike. They would set off into the bitterly cold night, little knowing that half-way across the world two people were hurtling through the thickening undergrowth, separated by anger, on the trail of gun-runners. Next week, it would be Christmas day. In Norfolk, her family would be sitting down to the usual heavy dinner, and opening presents. Where would she be? Judging by the present state of affairs, still forcing her unwelcome company on this accident-prone South African!

The track forked just ahead of them and Jan had to slow down to decide which branch to take. In fact, he stopped and got out to inspect the ground for evidence, and Margaret watched him thoughtfully. If there was one good thing which had come out of their misfortune it was that she was beginning to understand him a little more. His eyes were still stormy when they slid across hers as he entered the cab, but she had the impression that her behaviour had been overshadowed by a worse source of anger. He swung off along the right-hand track which headed into wilder solitary landscape, and a mile or so further on it narrowed into nothingness which meant they were driving over grass and dodging trees.

Margaret was just wondering how Jan knew he was going in the right direction when her attention was caught by a clownish face peering over the top of a tree.

"Oh Jan, look . . . a giraffe! And there are more!" she added excitedly. "Aren't they the most interesting animals you have ever seen! I have been waiting nearly a year for this. Do stop for a minute and . . ." She turned to him and her voice tailed off as she remembered the circumstances which had defeated her ambition to work here.

"We're not on a sight-seeing trip," he grunted.

After that she contented herself with watching absorbedly from the window trying to photo-memorize all she saw to bring out again when she had the time to enjoy it. The giraffes had broken into an ungainly canter as the truck rushed past, and she had smiled to herself at the sight. There was a large herd of wildebeest and zebra grazing together as they often did, and any amount of buck ranging from the miniature exquisite steenbuck to the various families of horse-sized but nevertheless delicate creatures which make up the whole endearing species. Most of these were only seen at a distance for Jan's approach was not designed for animal-spotting, and the racing vehicle scared them. Margaret longed to ply him with questions which she was sure he would willingly have answered under different circumstances.

The vast array of birds was too active for her to recognize any although her knowledge of African species was very limited. The vivid colours and strangely compelling cries were enough to content her that day, and new hope that she might return at a later date added to her gladness at the sight of them. Then, at last, came the sight every visitor to Africa longs for. Jan spotted them first and slowed to a crawl. He said nothing, but Margaret detected a look of pride on his face when she breathed, "They really are the royalty of the animal kingdom!"

She had turned to look from the window on his side of the cab as they slid past a small group of lions sitting like assembled statuary with the ascending sun burnishing their coats to luminous gold. The animals regarded the truck with sleepy slit eyes and compressed mouths in their tawny muzzles. To Margaret they appeared to be saying, "Yes, you are passing unmolested because we are too lazy to do anything about it. Come again tomorrow and it might be a different matter!" As if to emphasize the fact, one lioness rolled over in slow motion throwing her giant paws above her head in a monster travesty of a playful puppy, but her companions remained squinting with deceptive watchfulness at the distance beyond.

Jan accelerated once they had passed the beasts and Margaret said, "Even if I have to return to England straight away, I shall be grateful for the last few minutes."

He kept his screwed-up eyes on the distance ahead. "Knowing you, I doubt if you will accept defeat so easily. Even if the opportunity to work at Myala falls through, no doubt you will be able to wangle a job in one of the other Reserves. Use that big-eyed technique on someone who doesn't know you and you'll get what you want."

She rounded on him. "All through our association you have condemned me as cold, yet you are equally bitter when I behave like the girls you admire so much!"

"It's your timing I deplore . . . and it was hardly worthy of good old, stiff upper-lip, true-blue Margaret Ward." He said the last in a fair imitation of her cultured tones. Unaccountably she coloured vividly. He had made her sound such a prig!

"Is it because I am English that you dislike me so much?" she asked curiously.

"I don't dislike Helen—she is English."

"What then?"

Since he had just been mentally listing all the justifiable reasons for his anger against her he brought it out pat, like a pre-flight instrument check.

"Practically your first words to me were that you had never had to struggle for anything in your life . . . it all came to you for the asking. I took you to Van Heerdon's party where you sat aloof like a psychiatrist observing the mentally-disturbed at play. You continued the theme at my flat."

"I didn't ask to go to that party!"

"Don't interrupt! You have a supremely over-estimated opinion of yourself with regard to the rest of the human race. They are simply there to be studied through your biologically microscopic eyes, and all their faults and weaknesses are noted with long-suffering forbearance. You, on the other hand, are blameless. Vices such as smoking, drinking, or bedding with a man play no part in *your* life. Your diet consists of all the health-giving foods, you cycle everywhere—since you never play love games, I suppose you have to get your exercise some other way—and no doubt you have never gone to sleep without cleaning your teeth and brushing your hair a hundred times.

"There has been no lack of evidence that you regard me as juvenile, dissolute and delinquent, and you jump up to protect me with maternal indignation when the law catches up with me, but it's time someone told you a man likes to fight his own battles rather than let a militant do-gooding female do it for him!"

"Now I know, I'll leave you to inject your own morphia and dress your own wounds as best you can," she put in shakily.

"Don't fling that at me," he snapped, taking his eyes from the bush and flicking them over her. "I am not talking about normal acts of humanity, and you know it! It's the tendency you have of treating me as a tiresome little boy who has to be pulled back on to the path of righteousness."

"If you didn't act like one, maybe I wouldn't respond that way," she cried. "I can't say I'm impressed with what I have seen so far!"

"I don't give a bloody damn! Compared with your pristine, fortune-favoured life, mine has been a never-ending struggle to make things happen the way *I* want them. Disappointments, set-backs, and strong competition tend to develop less than praiseworthy traits in a person, but even if I had been born with a silver spoon in my mouth, I hope I wouldn't have grown up as insufferably perfect as you!"

Margaret's cheeks were flaming by now. "Losing your temper and insulting me only proves my point. A *man* wouldn't react in this way."

"You've got it all wrong, Miss Purity. A *man* is not necessarily a *gentleman*. My brothers are all *men*, but regularly lose their tempers. Ask anyone!"

"Ah, but you are not like your brothers . . . you have already told me. And *that* is the root of all the trouble, isn't it?" she thrust at him. "You have never forgotten the rough time they gave you as a boy, and read continued persecution into everything they say or do. If *I* have grown-up insufferably perfect, *you* have grown-up insufferably martyred. From what I hear, the rest of the family is heartily sick of your puerile histrionics of late."

"Who told you that?" he shouted, stamping on the brake.

"Helen," she shouted back, "and when they hear of this latest idiocy they really will cast you out. You have ruined Chris, and they won't tolerate a Judas among their number."

"If you were a man I'd hit you for that," he grated out through whitened lips.

"If *you* were a man, you would," she cried, bursting into tears. Why didn't he strike her? What she had said was appalling. Suddenly, in adding the facets to the gem of her life, Destiny's edge had slipped and cut a little too deeply. The quarrel had avalanched alarmingly and Margaret, a novice at impassioned anger, had been unable to stay the course with any sort of control. Never in her life had she flayed anyone with her tongue in that manner . . . it was completely foreign to her nature. Or was it? Perhaps there was a lot more locked away inside her waiting for the provocation to draw it out!

The sobbing continued as she leant her aching head against the side of the cab. Oh, he was right; she had been living like one of the experimental mice she had worked on. Enclosed in a glass case of respect-ability, her every action had been predictable and channelled correctly by those around her so that she had no idea of the depths of the human jungle outside. Who was she to point a condemnatory finger at anyone—least of all Jan? What did she know of his life? All she had to go on were a few words of Helen's and the evidence of three days spent with him.

In retrospect she now saw his behaviour not as juvenile, but courageous . . . impulsively so, but courageous nevertheless. By flying that Dakota he had been prepared to risk Chris's anger to prove what his brother would not believe by persuasion, and he had accepted the blow dealt him by ill-fortune without wailing or gnashing of teeth. There was no doubt that Sergeant De Wet back at Alwynsrus was a bigger rogue than the man he had imprisoned, and Jan had been right to break out from that prison cell. The tangle with Craig and Co. was better described as foolhardiness than courage, but to chase after them, knowing the odds were three to one, was not the action of a delinquent. And all this without hope of coming out of the affair with any credit for himself! She wiped her eyes and reflected miserably that she had not even committed the crime of using mascara which would run down her cheeks to prove she was human!

Jan had climbed from the truck and was flexing the tenseness from his body as he gazed around him. The pain in his stomach had increased since that girl had revealed that she and Helen had been discussing him that day at Sea Point. He had thought better of his sister-in-law! How well he remembered the indignity of having his two sisters prying into his secrets and rushing to tell anyone who cared to listen, then when he set on them and was severely taken to task for hitting girls, they stood giggling just out of reach.

He had even once been put in their charge when his brothers had all gone down with a stomach upset after drinking Chris's home-brewed beer. He had suffered taunts from the boys, then. While *they* had been suffering from the results of a manly experiment, *he* had to be looked after by feminine nursemaids! How he had longed to lay into all four of them—had started, until Chris had told him not to be a young idiot and hauled him away. Even now, fond though he was of his sisters, the least suggestion of their interference in his life brought forth a firm directive to keep their pretty noses out. The knowledge that Chris's wife had chewed him over with a comparative stranger hit him hard. Helen had always seemed to be more understanding than most people and he had trusted her. That was women for you! They changed personalities without any warning.

Take this girl, for instance. The tears flowing so freely down her cheeks surprised him until a momentary recollection of "tipsy Maggie" returned, reminding him she could succumb to weakness. Now his anger had been vented he felt empty. It was not his custom to be boorish to women, but with his life in such a mess at the moment if he *had* to have a woman on his hands he would have preferred the usual type. Still he should know by now that obstacles leapt up at every turning where he was concerned. With a sigh he returned to the cab to take down one of the water bottles.

"Drink?" he offered to the girl, ignoring her distress.

She took it automatically and held it clasped on her lap.

"The idea is to unscrew the top and

guzzle," he said, taking it back and opening it. "Here."

"Thank you." The words came out very thickly.

After she had quenched her thirst Jan took a good pull at the water to wash the dust from his throat. There was still a fair distance to go and he didn't want to halt again. His eyes roamed the distance, looking for inspiration, but there was only the parched bush against coppery sky; the growth of Africa which had been there before his birth and would be there long after he was forgotten. Somewhere along that perimeter fence there had to be an access to the neighbouring country, and unless they had a giant crane handy, Craig would have to leave the jeep this side. Everything depended on how quickly he found it and traced the spot where Craig had crossed over. He pulled himself back into the cab and switched on the engine, but was brought from his thoughts by the girl beside him.

"Jan."

"Yes."

"Do you think you could strike my remarks from your memory? My only excuse is that I am very inexperienced at quarrelling and lost sight of the rules. I truly didn't mean the bit about your being a Judas."

"I know you didn't," he said surprisingly. "You wouldn't be vitriolic to someone you persist in mothering, but it struck just a bit too near home for my conscience."

The truck leapt forward, cutting short any further inroads into the quarrel and she took his hint, contenting herself by asking how he knew where to go. When he explained, she faced him with what he proposed doing when he found the abandoned jeep.

"I shall cross the border after them. You can take the truck back to headquarters."

"When and if you catch Craig, you surely don't expect them to surrender quietly. Once they are over the border I imagine South African law cannot touch them without an extradition order."

His mouth twisted into a wry smile. "That is too elevated an idea of my motives. I have no noble desire to serve the ends of justice by marching three miserable men to the nearest police station single-handed.

My sole purpose is to obtain the names of everyone involved in this business and a written statement from each of them declaring that Chris had no part in it. I'll break them in two to get it, if necessary, but as far as justice goes, they'll snare themselves in a net of their own making, given time."

"Why didn't you twist Craig's arm when you had the chance?"

"I only *suspected* him; I had nothing to back my belief until he ran. There was only one name I was sure of, and I'm saving him till last."

"Van Heerdon?"

He nodded.

"I don't think you'll intimidate *him* enough to do your bidding. He is a vulture who lives off the carcase of society . . . and who can prey on a vulture?"

The question was never answered because a large grey mass emerged from the trees right into their path making Jan screech to a halt. The elephant was a huge bull with madly flapping ears and villainous under-sized eyes, who was leading a small herd through the bush along one of their recognized routes. Jan knew enough to stop and wait for them to pass.

"Don't move," he told Margaret. "They have a worse temper than mine."

She was thrilled and fascinated to see them lumber on their way, uprooting trees and crashing with giant feet through the scrub, but she saw them with the eyes of a *uitlander*, and knew nothing of how dangerous they could be if somebody blocked the path. This encounter with Jumbo prompted Jan to turn into an intensely interesting guide, pointing out creatures she would have missed and telling her facts about South Africa which intrigued and sometimes angered her. As he spoke, he revealed a true and serious love of his homeland which fell gladly on the ears of a girl used to the throw-away, deprecatory staunchness of the average Englishman, and showed her another side of his character. But then, he would be as loyal to his country as his family, she reasoned. Would he also be as unwaveringly faithful to the woman he married? Her protective instinct for this man was momentarily pierced by the fear of his deep, dedicated love being wounded by a woman who treated it carelessly. Should he survive all else, *that* she felt sure would be the finish of him.

It was mid-morning and very hot before Jan's expert eyes spotted the fence which bounded the Reserve. He drove to it and pulled up.

"Have another drink while I take a look around," he advised the girl as he lit a cigarette. "It's a question of deciding whether to go north or south."

"Is there anything to eat? I'm starving!"

"There's fruit, cheese and biscuits in that box. Take pity on the driver and don't eat it all." The smile was a surprise. She had not seen him do it all that often, and the warmth and spontaneity of this one brought her close to him in one giant leap—metaphorically, not physically, because he limped away to examine the perimeter track for any clues. It was only an outside chance. Craig might have his access gate miles from this particular spot and they could easily waste time driving in the opposite direction.

Margaret armed herself with oat biscuits, cheese and an apple and wandered across to the shade of some trees to eat the strange breakfast. During the drive the sun had been biting into her arms and, although she didn't burn as a rule, the worst her skin had been subjected to was the mid-summer blaze at the Cornish holiday home owned by her parents . . . a far cry from the searing heat of the *veld*. As she munched, her thoughts flew seven thousand miles to the scene of their annual family retreat to the West Country and saw again the familiar pattern of the three weeks they spent there. They had been joining forces with a neighbouring holiday family of equal middle-class wealth and respectability for many years, Margaret and her sister playing with their two sons when children, making light, flirtatious love with them as the years passed. While the young people were out dancing or walking hand in hand along the moonlit shore, their elders played canasta or bridge, secure in the knowledge that the friendship between the boys and girls would never go beyond what was expected of them. It was idyllic . . . and looking back on it now, predictably *dull*! Margaret pushed back her heavy hair in frustration. No, she would not return to it just yet. As

Jan suggested, there must surely be other opportunities for her in South Africa!

Busy with possible plans for her future, her attention was suddenly drawn by a slight movement above her. Through the dry leaves on the branch slightly to her left, a bright green smooth body was visible as it slid along with regular expanding and contracting movements. It was a sight to set a person's blood running cold, especially when she had no means of defence. The snake had spotted Margaret and froze, but it could not have been more still than the girl rooted to the spot below.

Jan returned along the path none the wiser as to which direction Craig had taken. It was still a fifty-fifty choice; one he would have to make *now*. The truck came into his view but he didn't immediately spot Margaret. When he did his reflexes leapt into alertness and his hand automatically reached for his revolver. A soft oath escaped him and he cast around for an alternative weapon. A broken limb from a tree provided the only solution, and since it was better than nothing, he grabbed it up and called softly to the girl, "Keep perfectly still and don't panic! I'm here now."

Schooling himself to edge forward inch by inch, he kept his gaze fixed on the jewel eyes and flicking tongue of the reptile. Margaret was not panicking, he noted, but seemed paralysed with fear. At last, he reached her and, holding the branch at the ready, put his left arm round her waist pulling her back against him. Step by step they backed away from the trees until they were far enough away for the snake to lose interest in its potential danger and slither away. As soon as this happened Margaret broke free and turned shining eyes to Jan.

"Why did you pull me away! That is the first chance I have had to see a *Boom slang* in its natural environment, and I was thrilled. I can't go back now; too much movement upsets them. They're not really dangerous, you know, as long as one keeps still."

Jan's expression defied description. He looked down at the flushed excited face beneath the floppy cotton sun-hat and experienced an emotion quite foreign to him. It was the first time he had wanted to wring a woman's neck! Unable to trust himself to speak, he flung down the branch and hobbled back to the truck, where he poured water down his throat and over his head to cool himself down in more ways than one. He was no naturalist. That snake could have been a green mamba—swift death in a smooth skin—but her superior knowledge had made his rescue bid appear melodramatic!

Margaret watched him in dismay. Would she never learn? It would not have been difficult to *pretend* she had been afraid. She was Queen Elizabeth flinging Raleigh's muddy cloak back in his face!

There seemed nothing to talk about after that. Jan ate his way through a huge square of cheese and three apples as the truck kicked up a dust trail behind them. If he had chosen the wrong direction they would have to drive back through it and, knowing his luck, it was more than likely. He was wrong. After half an hour he spotted the jeep half-concealed by trees about a hundred yards from the boundary fence. He drew up alongside it and levered himself out. It took him twenty minutes of searching before he found the cunning "door" in the fence where the cuts in the wire had been covered with grey rubber to disguise any sign of tampering from the

Rangers who regularly inspected the boundary confines. He returned to the truck, pocketed a couple of apples, slung two water bottles over his shoulder and looked at Margaret.

"*Tot siens!*" He sketched a salute and turned away.

"Jan, I haven't the faintest idea how to get back."

He stopped with his back to her and she waited with a bumping heart for him to turn to face her, but he didn't. "You go back to the spot where we saw the snake, then head west until you reach that fork in the track."

If she looked wide-eyed and helpless it was real this time.

"I'd never make it. I was too busy looking at the animals to notice where you were going, and navigation is one of my failures. I even lose myself at home . . . it's quite a joke."

He turned then with his eyes closed in an attempt to keep his temper. "It doesn't strike me as funny. Don't play stupid games at this stage."

"I mean it, Jan. I'll drive around until the petrol runs out and still be lost."

It would seem to be a stalemate, but Jan was well used to easing out of tricky situations and inspiration came at the right time. In the jeep left behind by Craig would be a two-way radio which linked with headquarters, so he could contact one of the Rangers to come out for the girl. This solution didn't appear to please Margaret because she turned about face when he explained it and claimed there was no need for him to do that, after all. Her protest was so vociferous he decided she had been leading him on all along, and pursued the subject no further.

Margaret was left standing beneath the sun, a small lonely figure with mixed-up feelings, as her only human link crossed into the neighbouring country and vanished into the trees. She had not dared let him contact headquarters for fear Chris had already arrived there, but by stopping him she had destroyed her only chance of returning. This Reserve covered around two and a half thousand square miles. What were the chances of her hitting the right track, and how long could she survive on two bottles of water, some cheese and an orange?

7

STRANGE bird-calls echoed across the ripe grasslands stretching around her, and the warm smell of vegetation, sweet and wild, settled into its previous heady blanket after the disturbance caused by the arrival of the truck. Away to the left the cry of beasts in flight was quickly stilled, leaving this corner of Africa to lie acquiescent while the blaze of day lived through its short reign until night dethroned it with soft persuasion.

Minutes passed, insignificant in the realms of the earth, but the most decisive in the life of one human soul upon it. There was a choice to be made quickly and irrevocably, and Margaret struggled with it. She could wait until a few hours before nightfall, then call up headquarters on the two-way radio (providing she discovered how to operate it) or she could follow Jan. There should be *no* choice; the only sensible decision was the first . . . Yet . . . ? Following that action to its probable conclusion she visualized the arrival of a jeep to escort her back, Chris or some provincial official arranging her immediate flight to Cape Town where she would either return to a January Norfolk, or go back several months later after frustrated attempts to arrange study at another Game Reserve.

Chris and Helen would be sincerely grateful for what she had done on Jan's behalf in the Dakota, but she would be shut out from any further part in the affair. The Schroeders closed ranks against outsiders when one of their number was in trouble and they would never forgive her for tricking Chris, then leaving Jan to go it alone without the support of his brother. Yes, it would be a polite "thank you" then a firmly closed door.

Wouldn't that be the best thing that had ever happened to her . . . to be shot of the man she had so recently condemned as insufferably martyred; to shake off the incisive influence which had begun to hack at the faceless jewel which had represented Margaret Ward from birth till three weeks ago? Flight from a lion was instinctive to all creatures who dared not confront him lest with a gun . . . yet it would be a sadly haunting sight to see him stilled and brought down. Maybe he had a reputation for aggression, but he was honest about it. The fact was presented for all the world to see; this is what I am and you must accept me! Not for him the sly "floating log" trick of the crocodile, the camouflaged "death in a tree" of the leopard, or the insinuating fatal embrace of the boa constrictor. The lion bounced into open grassland, throwing down his gauntlet with a deafening roar. He was fearless, beholden to no one, yet fiercely loyal to the members of his own pride whom he would defend against all odds.

There had never been any question of what she would do, Margaret decided as she slung the water bottles over her shoulder and crossed to the wire fence. Jan had lambasted her with the truth about her glib acceptance of a fairy-godmother life without knowing that the past three days had tarnished the tinsel, setting up an ache of restlessness which would intensify if she obeyed her commonsense. The spell of Africa must be on her, driving her from the cocoon to face whatever was waiting

. . . and if she fell by the wayside in the process, it would be better than remaining in frozen transition inside—neither one thing nor the other!

She did not bother to disguise the "gate" again as Jan had. The two vehicles would be found, and whoever searched for the access would find it more easily. A path saved her the bother of choosing the right direction, but it was not so well-defined that she didn't find herself pushing the undergrowth aside and stumbling over small obstacles. Within minutes she was hot and sweating, and not a little alarmed. Jan could only have had ten minutes' start on her, but with his longer stride and familiarity with this type of terrain he might be way, way ahead by now. The vegetation was too dense to allow a distant view so there was no way of telling if the path branched off. An immediate doubt of the wisdom of what she had done was pushed down by an equally swift counter-thought. "Drooping wings already," said an inner voice. "How will you ever learn to fly?"

Half an hour of dogged pushing and scrambling lengthened into an hour. The path had not diverted, but neither had she had any sign of the man ahead and her resolution was definitely weakening. Afraid of dropping even further behind, Margaret uncorked the water bottle and took quick sips as she kept on walking, but it was her undoing. A tangled knot sent her sprawling and she watched the precious water trickle into the thirsty earth. It was not her last; she still had the other bottle, but there was no way of knowing how soon she would meet up with Jan. Back on her feet, she pushed on with renewed effort. If Jan could keep going after the beating he received this morning, and on an injured leg, then so could she!

Margaret had taken no account of Jan's greater strength and driving anger inside him which deadened all physical pain as he ploughed on. The girl had been dismissed from his thoughts soon after leaving her, so sure had he been that she had given up her silly game and was now on her way to headquarters. Under his breath he called her what he felt he should have called her to her face, and thanked Providence he was now rid of her. Whoever arrived in answer to the Ranger's radio-telephone call would get her safely back to Cape Town where she could sort herself out. One thing was absolutely sure . . . she would fall on her feet, that one. A thrusting memory of "tipsy Maggie" and her glowing face as she had watched the lions earlier today was trodden firmly underfoot by the mortification he had felt over the snake episode. Oh yes, that girl was supremely capable of returning unscathed to the bosom of her family—they were welcome to her!

From experience, he guessed the path he was following led to a native *kraal*. From there he would discover where Craig Barker and the two Rangers were headed. It would not be to a city, that much was certain. Rebel guerrillas had their headquarters out in the wild from where they made surprise raids before vanishing into the hide-out once more. With luck, the inhabitants of the *kraal* ahead would have knowledge of the actual headquarters, and if he played his cards right, it might be possible to coax the information from them.

Craig had panicked and run, but his action would betray his associates. They would not be too pleased about that! Those crates of guns at Alwynsrus would also prove a thorn in their sides. Unless his judgement of character was sadly wrong, Jan felt certain Sergeant De Wet would keep quiet about his discovery, but he was also the type of man who was never satisfied and would definitely like to be assured that there were more where these had come from in return for his silence. Craig and his masters would also suspect this. Jan didn't give much for the drunken sergeant's chances if they did!

The memory of the punishing blows Craig had dealt him that morning fanned the heat of his anger anew. It was a long time since he had been outnumbered that way, but it still sparked in him the desire for revenge. Contempt for this type of unfair fight was tempered by the fact that Craig could have killed him had he wished. That must surely prove that he had no hand in the murder of Russell Martin. Whatever kind of villain the Assistant Warden was, he was no killer! Jan was at a loss to know how or why Craig had allowed himself to become involved in this affair, then with a flood of guilt, remembered his own lemming-like association with Van Heerdon. He had no right to condemn similar actions in another fool!

Russell Martin must have discovered Craig's sideline just as this consignment was due in, and the receivers on this side of the border must have dealt with him. The manner of his murder suggested native African involvement, but there surely must be a big white boss! He had no idea how long it would take the Provincial authorities to garner all the facts brought to light by Dr. Martin's death and get around to the part played by Schroeder Freight, but in that time he intended gathering enough evidence to clear Chris when the moment of reckoning came.

Van Heerdon would be easy. The threat to reveal places and dates of when he had picked up mystery passengers, plus details and destinations of doubtful cargoes transported during the past years should be sufficient pressure to gain what he wanted. He was in enough trouble himself not to hesitate over revealing further incriminating evidence, and Van Heerdon would know that. Craig, if separated from his bully boys, could be intimidated into signing anything. The stumbling block would be the man in charge of the operation on this side. Jan had no lever with which to prise co-operation from him, but as surely as the sun would set tonight, he would find one.

These violent thoughts so possessed him it was some time before he became aware of the flanking escort he had acquired. His first reaction was not one of alarm. Natives from bush *kraals* were not hostile as a rule; indeed, many a white man or woman had been given hospitality and willing assistance when they had strayed into the territory by mistake, and Jan looked upon the six black warriors as inquisitive fellow-travellers. He spoke to them in English, and when there was no response, tried Afrikaans with the same negative result. The several greeting phrases which were all he knew of native tongues brought no better success, which surprised him. Unless these men came from a little-known tribe, they should have known *one* of the expressions of friendship he had used.

A frown settled on his forehead as he studied his companions. Shorter than a lot of Africans, they nevertheless moved with the easy grace of the black man. Each wore a sporran of animal hide and various bead ornaments to decorate his limbs, but the assegais they carried looked as deadly a weapon as any tribal spear. There was nothing in their manner to suggest enmity, but when Jan halted to light a cigarette they converged on him.

The match was never struck and the cigarette was plucked from his fingers and thrown on the ground. It was pointless to try any kind of resistance, but he felt sick with disgust at how easily he had walked into the trap. Craig must have known it was simply a matter of time before he was trailed across the border—and this was the reception committee. He cursed himself for being such a babe in the ways of the criminal to believe all he had to do was negotiate his terms for keeping silent. His original idea of a large organization being behind the gun-running was correct—bigger than he had imagined, probably—and they would look upon him as a suicidal fool for coming here alone and unarmed. It spoke volumes for his innocence of crime that he had not realized that, once having used him, Van Heerdon would never let him go; had known his temperament well enough to be sure he would toe the line if it came to a threat to Schroeder Freight.

With his wrists fastened behind his back with thin cord, he moved off, encircled by his captors. Now oppression brought a return of all pain. The familiar tearing sensation in his thigh was joined by an ache from his battered abdomen, and a throbbing jaw. For an instant his fingers curled into tight fists behind him as he remembered the way Craig had let into him earlier that day, but it was an impotent gesture for a man rendered helpless.

Fifteen minutes or so had passed when he was suddenly dragged from the path into surrounding trees and was shocked into the belief that his life was about to end. Certainly, the natives held their assegais at threatening angles, but when several moments went by without further action, Jan suspected the black men had heard sounds which had been inaudible to his less acute hearing.

Sure enough, he was relieved to pick up the give-away cracking of twigs which heralded the arrival of whoever was pursuing them, but when Margaret came into view, clothes torn and stained by vegetation, bare arms scratched, and her mutinous face red with exertion, Jan groaned and recited his complete vocabulary of invective under his breath.

When the tribesmen moved out from their cover Margaret screamed. In the main, she would not be afraid of natives, but she was at the end of her tether. To a fastidious person, a battle through humid, thorny undergrowth which tore at her hair and clothes and caused her to sweat profusely, besides covering her with insect bites, was the last straw to already severely tested nerves. The unexpected appearance of these dark-skinned warriors brought the cry before she was aware of making it and, for once, she didn't know how to deal with a situation. Before the problem became urgent, Jan was dragged from concealment and finished off her wretchedness by saying, "You have helped no one by doing this, least of all yourself. You won't find these people as tolerant of your wilfulness as I am."

In another situation she would have laughed hysterically at that—intolerance was one of his biggest faults—but his sinister message got through to her all right. The skilful fencing she had used to counteract his attacks on her would be completely ineffective on the native temperament and mind. She was not to know that in most cases there would be nothing to fear from the inhabitants of the many *kraals* in the vast wilderness of Africa, so the sight of Jan as their prisoner raised naked fear such as she had never felt before.

It was much too late to wish she had stayed at Myala to wait for Chris who would plan exactly what to do on behalf of his brother. Chris knew his own country, knew the people, and most of all, knew Jan . . . or did he? Did anyone know Jan? Was there one single person who could say for sure what was going through his mind as he limped along the path ahead of her? Was he letting off silent steam about what she had done, or had he dismissed her from his mind as he had on other occasions? Was he full of despair over his present situation, or did that mutinous spirit still burn brightly? Did he care at all what happened to her, or was he as unfeeling and insensitive to her fate as he made out?

The biologically-trained mind which Jan

had censured told her that a temperament which was fiery in anger and loyalty would also reflect that intensity in other emotions. Could such a man be totally disinterested in the safety of a woman threatened by danger, even though she had foolishly precipitated it against his advice? For herself, a relatively calm person, *his* welfare concerned her to an overwhelming degree, so surely he could not shrug this off as simply receiving her just desert! Stories of vile, hideous tribal punishments had penetrated even to her Norfolk village, and before long walking was made difficult by the violent trembling of her legs.

The sight of the *kraal* set in a clearing brought an increase of panic, but she fought valiantly to control the impulse to run to Jan. It might endanger his safety even more, although by that time the certainty that they were both about to die a cruel death had taken command of every other thought.

Their approach had been noted and the remaining tribesmen spilled from the circle of thatched huts to line the path which led into the centre of this small African village, and they goggled silently at the sight of a white man being brought in this way. Motivated by the desire to show off, one of the escorting warriors prodded Jan in the manner of a herdsman with a slothful beast, and caused him to stumble. Barely in time, Margaret clamped her lips over a cry of protest. A man liked to fight his own battles, Jan had told her. It was different for a woman. Just at the moment she would give up her career and all it entailed for a little help.

Slowly the procession moved down through the opening in the stockade of stout pointed saplings until it burst into a central clearing surrounded by huts. It was a fairly typical *kraal*, which surprised Margaret with its cleanliness. The primitive homes, some round, some square, had mud walls baked and bleached by the sun, in which were unpaned windows and a doorless entrance. Outside many of them were small fires with cooking pots on the boil, earthenware crocks or paraffin tins filled with water, signs of primitive threshing, and half-finished articles made from coloured beads. There was no sign of the women who might be expected to do this work. From the little Margaret knew, it was the female section of these communities which tackled the chores while their menfolk went hunting, or left for jobs in the big cities, so it was a surprise to find the place deserted. A mangy dog or two scavenged listlessly around the huts, but not a child or its mother was in sight.

Jan was taken to the centre of the clearing by four of the men while the remaining two pushed Margaret towards one of the huts and with threatening gestures forced her to go in. There was nothing inside to warrant the thumping of her heart; all it held was a couple of rush mats with bright wool blankets folded at the head. The floor was swept clean and the walls were frost-white, but the atmosphere inside was the reverse of a refrigerator. An instant reminder of her claustrophobic ordeal inside the Dakota turned her on her heel with the intention of running into the open once more, but the doorway was guarded either side by the tribesmen who had no intention of letting her free. She stood, clutching her skirt, trying to regain control of her composure. Three days and nights as Jan's sole companion had left her feeling bereft without him, and the dread of what these people might do to them precipitated the longing to be by his side when they faced it.

Through the opening she watched as a rope collar was slipped over Jan's head and fastened, neatly but not tightly, round his neck. The other end was secured to a peg driven in the dry earth so that he stood in the centre of the clearing, his hands tied behind his back, tethered like an animal. The men of the *kraal* slowly gathered in a circle around their prisoner and began a melancholy chanting while they swayed back and forth with mesmeric movements. Jan had his back to her so Margaret could not even draw strength from visual contact with him, and a burning impotence began growing within her.

The chanting grew louder and louder to reach a crescendo which tightened Margaret's nerves to breaking point, when the reason for all this build-up appeared. Through the trees leapt the star of the show; a giant of a man decked out in feather wings, with vivid body paintings and a face-mask which represented a grotesque bird-like head. A roar went up and the black men all retreated several paces before

225

silence fell on the scene, leaving the bird man holding centre stage. For effect, he strutted round the gathered audience, taking no notice of the man tethered a few feet away, and Margaret took a good look at him. The size and height he commanded was an illusion built up by the trappings he wore. The huge beaky mask was designed to rise a foot above the top of his head and several times wider than a normal human face, but it looked in proportion to the massive shoulders produced by the cunning feather wings which arched out like a vulture's. Above his knees were bands which held feather "stockings" which hung to the ground like the fluffy legs of a fighting cock, and a similar decoration covered his arms from the elbow down. Even the way he walked and moved was designed to suggest a bird of prey and it was obvious to Margaret that here was that much-feared figure, the tribal witch-doctor!

The parade over, he took his stand beside the prisoner and Margaret witnessed the power of gifted oration. Without understanding a word that was said, the wild arm-waving and cavortions looked ridiculously melodramatic, but she had seen teenage fans worked up to a dangerous pitch by similar performances by pop-stars, and knew he held his audience completely captive. It seemed the whole impassioned speech concerned the white man, because this tribal charlatan made repeated aggressive gestures at him which caused his followers to copy them. While the inhabitants of the *kraal* stamped their feet restlessly and set up great shouts at regular intervals, their leader leapt higher and higher and whirled ever closer to Jan until he suddenly reached out to grab him by the hair. The movement pulled the rope collar tighter and the watching girl pressed her fingers to her mouth in silent agitation.

When it became clear Jan was not about to have his head wrenched from his shoulders, the ugly pantomime began to have some meaning. The colour of his hair was the subject under review! Beneath the twelve o'clock sun it shone with fiery lights; a single glowing ember amongst the black coals encircling it, and this man was cursing Jan because of it. Amongst white people a red-head was worthy of comment; here, where everyone had a black matted busby of hair, he was a freak—bad medicine!

Using this physical attribute to his advantage, the witch-doctor made mystic signs and symbolic gestures as he strutted round and round his subject, and the assembled tribesmen quickly worked up a frightening antipathy towards Jan. Despite this, they kept at a safe distance from the supposed evil of the man with the burning hair.

The whole scene was beginning to mesmerize Margaret. Rhythmic stamping feet, glistening ebony bodies swaying in unison, and monotonous chanting all had a somnolent effect on her until she pulled herself up, sharply recognizing it for what it was—mass hypnosis. Next minute, above the chanting, came a sound like heavy water falling on to stone. The tribesmen cringed in mortal fear as they fell silent at the long eerie wail which left the lips of the bird-figure. Margaret craned her head forward through the window aperture in an attempt to follow his pointing finger, then drew in a startled breath. On the far side of the compound the thatched roof of one of the huts was afire, the flames devouring the dry grass with crackling, spluttering gluttony and shooting a spiral of smoke upwards to the sun.

It was the magnificent finale of the tribal magician, a masterly display of sorcery by one who had studied his subject and his audience to an uncanny degree. With advance knowledge of Jan's arrival, the witch-doctor had had time to prepare his strategy. It was not difficult to start a fire in tinder-dry grass under this fierce heat. The application of a small fragment of glass or inflammatory material was all that was needed to produce this spectacular evidence of Jan's affinity with the element of fire. Margaret could only marvel, but the others present saw it as a manifestation of wickedness which could destroy them. From that minute, there was not a warrior amongst them who did not look upon this white man as his enemy!

Having achieved his object, the bird-figure departed and the circle gradually broke up, leaving Jan alone. For five minutes Margaret waited for the next development, but when they lengthened into ten and the normal routine of the *kraal* began again with the women and children leaving their hiding places in the huts, the dreadful truth dawned on her. The wives and young adolescent girls took up their chores with sublime indifference to the stranger in their midst, and naked liquorice children continued another day of indolent happiness with their simple playthings. Only when one bold infant approached too near the white man did his mother show that she was aware of his presence by commanding her offspring to return to her side immediately. Jan was left, a solitary figure isolated in the midst of a busy community, and there they planned to leave him beneath the burning sky as if he were of no more account than one of the skinny bleating goats which were tethered beside their homes.

The scene stood out in frightening 3–D, and it was more than the girl could bear. She rushed at the doorway, but the guards were too quick for her and barred the entrance.

"You can't leave him there," she shrieked at them. "Let me go to him . . . at least let me be *with* him."

They forced her back into the interior, but when a woman is desperate she makes a powerful adversary. "Look, look," she gasped, fumbling in her bag. "Look, you can have these." Her trembling fingers offered a small mirror and nail scissors, but when these were met with a dumb stare, flung them down and produced a platinum ball-point pen and a mother-of-pearl compact. "Go on . . . take them!" she commanded wildly. "You can have the lot. Just let me out of here. I've got to get out, do you hear. OUT!" Another rush was met with similar resistance, so she changed her tactics and tackled the window aperture. It was impossible to squeeze through so small a square, but through it she could see Jan with that vile rope collar rooting him to the spot, and passion flared anew.

"He'll die if you leave him there! Don't you understand, you savages, *that man will die*!" She didn't consider for a minute she was wasting her time addressing these men in English; there was simply a driving need to din the facts into their woolly heads. "Take me to that bird-man of yours," she pleaded desperately. "I'll pay you." Yanking open her purse she emptied the contents into her hand and held it out to them. After a few seconds of indecision, they took the notes with long sinewy fingers, and Margaret breathed her relief. It was short-lived! The tribesmen had no intention of letting her set foot outside that hut, as she discovered when they raised their assegais.

The last tattered remnants of her self-control deserted her and she turned into a lioness rather than a woman in her frenzied struggle to get to Jan. It met with impossible resistance, and she eventually flung herself against an interior wall with an hysterical sob of surrender.

"Oh no, no, no!" The palms of her hands banged against the hard-baked mud. "Oh no, no!"

The tears flowed fast and unheeded as she sank to the ground, beside herself with distress, and buried her face against her bent-up knees while her hands, tugging at the shining hair falling each side of her face, sought to produce a pain more acute than that which was eating at her stomach. Never having been driven to such depth of feeling before, it was difficult for the girl to find an outlet, and between rasping sobs the words "Oh no, no" were repeated over and over again as she moved around the floor like one possessed.

During this time a kaleidoscope of memories floated through her brain with tormenting clarity. Jan, hurt and angry, telling Chris about the Dakota . . . Van Heerdon saying, "I can buy Jan any time I like" . . . her own pure tones: "There is nothing more fatal to the male of the species" . . . The shuddering and thumping of a plane landing in rough country . . . Jan saying, "Not another of those cattle injections" . . . black faces in the dimmed hospital lights . . . Sergeant De Wet leering and scratching his vast belly . . . trying to wake an amorous red-haired man in the middle of the night . . . the lions staring at her with unreadable expressions . . . Jan's freckled face bearing that same expression after she had grace-lessly chided him for rescuing her from the snake. *That* memory brought on a fresh need for punishment and she clawed at the floor breaking her nails in the process.

This was the moment of truth! After the first exploratory facets, the time had come for Destiny to make the final bold stroke which would cleave the jewel and hope to produce a perfect solitaire. Now, at last, there was something she wanted so badly she would fight for it against all odds; something which meant more to her than she had ever thought possible. Never had her heart's desire been so out of reach, so deep in the jungle, so lost in the rapids. This love for Jan had joined the conspiracy against her by arriving too late. No longer was she fooled by the adjectives "maternal" or "nursy", but recognized the surging inside her for what it was. No more did she wish to rap his knuckles or catechize over his smoking habits, nor did she have the urge to tuck him up in bed with a bandage round his head. Her one desire was to run out there and tell him that she understood what he had tried to do, that she believed in him, that here was someone who would stand by him no matter what he took on. The birth-pangs of this love were exquisite though they tore her apart, and her crying gradually diminished as the strength of it coursed through her veins.

Back at the window with some idea of fortifying him with a flow of telepathic compassion until she could devise a way of getting free, Margaret found him standing still as a rock with his head tilted up to some remote spot in the distance. The back of his shirt was wet through and his arms glistened with sweat, but there was no sign of flagging in his straight back. He was going through this without help, as he did with everything else! Her new perceptiveness shone into the depths of his character, revealing something which had always been there but which everyone seemed to have overlooked. Basically Jan Schroeder was a lonely man—and never more lonely than at this moment!

She gripped the white wall as the yearning built up once more within her, but before it reached ignition point, a white man emerged from behind the burnt-out hut and strolled across the compound. He was instantly recognizable as Elliot Van Heerdon.

8

"THANK GOD!" breathed Margaret as Van Heerdon reached Jan, but the newcomer made no attempt to release the captive. The girl watched incredulously as the pale, sandy-haired man stood conversing as if he were with a contemporary in a bar, paying no heed to the condition his listener was in. This man must be a real brute; he could not be excused as an uncivilized native under the spell of a superior intelligence. The sadistic trait which could leave another human to suffer while he looked on was deliberate and strong in him. The proof of this was when he started to walk away after repeated head-shakings from Jan—but he had reckoned without Margaret.

"I want a word with you," she cried, "or do you extend your brutality to women also!"

From his reaction it was clear he had had no idea of her presence. Spinning on his heel as his eyes searched wildly for the

236

source of this female voice speaking English, he gave every evidence of having received a severe shock, and Margaret took advantage of it.

"See how vulnerable you are," she taunted. "You may render one adversary helpless, but there is always another watching when you least expect it."

Van Heerdon located her then and came across to the window, even paler than before. "What are you doing here?" he demanded on an outgoing breath. "Nobody informed me of this."

"Your organization cannot be as trust-worthy as you thought. Sorry, but you have me on your hands and conscience whether you like it or not. The last time we met, you accused me of making you feel uncomfortable. I hope I have succeeded in doing it again!"

Van Heerdon came round to the doorway and the guards stood aside to let him enter. He looked at the girl in her dirt-smeared clothes and rubbed his chin nervously. "Craig Barker said you were at Myala, but I hadn't bargained on Jan bringing you with him. You are an unwelcome complication."

Suddenly Margaret's bravado vanished.

"You can't leave him out there . . . it's inhuman! Are you prepared to let a fellow man slowly die of heat and thirst while he is tied up like a lowly animal?"

A shadow flitted across the pale features. "Of course I shan't let him die. He is far too valuable!"

"Then why . . . ?"

"The minute he agrees to my proposition, that rope comes off."

"Proposition?"

"He has always been so amenable in the past. I can't understand this sudden vindictiveness."

"I told you you had not looked beneath his party manner."

"Quite the amateur psychologist, aren't you?" he sneered. "I suppose being an animal doctor entitles you to look upon the human race as the most sophisticated of the mammals, and pronounce on its behaviour." His plummy English accent sounded alien after three days surrounded by South Africans.

She realized she would get nowhere by arguing with him, and meanwhile Jan was out there beneath that sun!

"You haven't explained about the proposition," she coaxed, veering on to a different tack. "Perhaps I could persuade him to agree."

"Why you?" he shot at her.

"We have become lovers . . . that's why he brought me with him." The lie came out pat, and if she felt a small sense of shock at what she had said it didn't show on her face.

"I . . . see," said Van Heerdon thoughtfully. "I've never known Jan to take a woman's advice before . . . but you are not the type of woman he usually associates with. Perhaps it'll work."

"I'll see that it does."

The pale, almost invisible, eyebrows rose at that and the watery blue irises beneath them expressed mild respect. "I can't say I have your wealth of confidence, but go ahead by all means."

"Well?" She waited in a fever of impatience.

"Jan has worked for me in a small way for over a year. It was never a secret that he needed the extra money I paid him to boost up his share of Schroeder Freight with a view to taking control of the company. He is ambitious, but frustrated

. . . and the combination of these two qualities is what I want in my employees. They
are prepared to set aside their scruples to
achieve their aims. However, one cannot
have the best of both worlds and the price
they have to pay for this opportunity is
complete loyalty to me. I recognize their
needs and freely reward their services with
financial generosity, but when there is a
slight breakdown involving some personal
risk, I do *not* expect them to whine about
the consequences and demand sworn statements to let them off the hook. I have no
time for rats who desert a ship the minute
a small leak has sprung."

It was intolerable to listen to all this and
Margaret had to bite her lip to avoid leaping
to Jan's defence.

"Come to the point," she begged.

"In time. The longer he stays out there,
the easier your task will be. Now, where
was I? When Jan was first introduced to me
I could scarcely believe my good fortune. A
pilot with the necessary attributes was who
I had been looking for for a long time. As
a bonus, he had his own small company
with its two aircraft. I had thought, once
having found the right man, I would

have to supply the machine for him, but Schroeder Freight was the ideal cover to disguise any link with me. The only snag seemed to be his brother, Chris, but once I realized how things stood between them the whole set-up was perfect. I approached him cautiously, but he was so eager he leapt at the bait before I had even cast the line. During the early months he carried out, to my complete satisfaction, every assignment I gave him, but when the chance of this arms contract came up I decided to keep him in ignorance of what he was doing until he was in sole control of the air-freight company. It wasn't that I intended using his services without paying for them—I rewarded him indirectly by selling him that Dakota at a ridiculous price, for instance —but the project was too important to risk his making Chris suspicious by an unguarded slip of the tongue."

"So what do you want me to do?" inserted Margaret tautly.

"I planned this whole organization with masterly thoroughness," he went on as if she hadn't spoken. "I had the customer over here, the supplier in Cape Town, and the means of transporting the merchandise.

All I needed was a contact at Myala to pass the stuff over the border."

He leant back against the wall and stretched his lips in a smile. "You know, it's amazing how easily people can be bought!" It seemed to be one of his favourite subjects. "Young Craig's weakness is women, so when he went to the city after weeks at Myala he liked to live it up. It didn't take him too long to agree to a little poaching in the Reserve by these boys here, for which he received a percentage of the profits . . . and after that, we had him nicely on the hook. It wasn't ideal—his nerves are not steady enough for this type of contract, which is why he panicked and ran instead of dealing with Jan at Myala. I don't think I can use him any more. Russell Martin's death has really unmanned him."

"But you still want Jan?"

"Naturally. Once he recovers his senses he will see the situation for what it really is—the chance of his lifetime! It is not often I regard any of my people as indispensable, but he is as close to that as I am prepared to go. I see no reason why things cannot go on as before. When Craig radioed from Myala I flew up immediately, but once here it occurred to me that all is not lost. The authorities will connect the flight of the Assistant Warden and two Rangers with the murder of Russell Martin—that is all. Once I leak a little evidence of Craig's poaching there will be no doubt in anyone's mind. There will be no reason to suspect any other activity."

"What about the police sergeant at Alwynsrus?"

"I have already sent someone to deal with him."

Margaret closed her lips firmly after that remark. She did not wish Dr. Gavascar to be "dealt with", and since she was the only person who knew *he* knew about the guns, it ensured his safety. If only she had told Chris the whole story over the radio-telephone yesterday afternoon! Van Heerdon was right . . . the gun-running would be completely unsuspected.

He continued. "I can install another contact at Myala once things have calmed down, and Jan can continue flying guns in."

"He'll never do that!" she cried without thinking.

"That's what *he* said . . . but you feel

you can persuade him," returned Van Heerdon, his eyes narrowing. "You *are* sure of success, I trust."

She covered up her slip with, "Yes, providing you offer him an extra incentive. He is taking a big risk bringing those crates past the authorities."

"I have already told you I am generous to my employees; my proposition is more than that. In view of the unique importance he commands, I am prepared to speed-up Jan's take-over of Schroeder Freight. A lump sum should provide the financial expedient, and a little conniving on my part will ensure that Chris becomes discredited, loses some of his best clients, and eventually faces financial ruin. With Jan running the company with a couple of hand-picked assistants, we could really go places. The business could be extended world-wide. The prospects are endless! Jan would achieve an otherwise impossible ambition, and my business would flourish. He will never have such a golden opportunity again . . . yet he told me to go to hell! If his stubbornness is due to greed he is wasting his time, for I don't go in for haggling. That's my offer. He can take it or leave it!"

"And if he refuses?"

"He won't. An hour or two out there will make him settle for my terms. However, your offer to talk some sense into him will cut the proceedings short and be doing me a favour. If we are going to work together, I'd prefer Jan not to start out feeling resentful. It clouds issues unnecessarily!"

How little Van Heerdon knows Jan, thought Margaret. I could never persuade him to agree to this . . . I wouldn't try . . . but once he is untied and in this hut we have a chance of escape. He did it once without much trouble, I dare say he can do it again. The most important thing is to get him out of that sun!

"I see your point," she said. "Leave Jan to me . . . he'll soon come round."

"Hmm," commented Van Heerdon, "that pure exterior is, as I guessed, a cover for a scheming intelligent mind. Right, go on out and get to work."

That was not what she had expected. Jan would tell her to go to hell also, and her meddling in his affairs would make him even more fractious. Worse, would be the humiliation he would feel at having to stand with that abomination round his neck while she spoke to him. No, she could not subject him to that even had there been any hope that he might listen to her.

"I said we were lovers, not queen and slave," she began. "A woman's ways of persuasion are not to rope a man to a peg and demand his surrender, they are infinitely more subtle . . . and leave him feeling not the least resentful." Where once these comments would have been expressed in clinical tones, her voice now grew warm and soft at the thought of what she was suggesting. "In other words, I need to get him alone in here. You know Jan," she gushed on, "he won't be rushed into anything, especially by a woman, but I can gradually work him round to accepting your terms without his realizing it wasn't his decision."

Van Heerdon wasn't happy, but saw the wisdom of her words. "I suppose you are right. I'll give you until sundown. If you fail, we'll try my way again tomorrow—even if it strains relationships somewhat!"

"Go and untie him. I'll have him eating out of my hand by your deadline."

Her anxiety had to continue a little longer, however.

"It is not a simple matter of untying him. First, I have to tell the witch-doctor so that he can give the order and not lose face with his people. He was seen to tether the evil spirit, and he must be the one to declare that the malevolence has temporarily left the white man's body. You see how child-like these people can be, yet it is a popular belief that a European way of life should not be denied them. I'll leave you to reflect on that while I negotiate."

It must have been a good fifteen minutes before sounds of excitement in the compound drew Margaret to the window. She had been sitting on one of the mats, unable to watch the scene outside until it was evident some action was forthcoming. Van Heerdon had kept his word. Amid great shouting, the witch-doctor's trusty henchmen ceremoniously removed the collar, and Jan was free! For a terrible moment, it seemed he was unable to move and Margaret willed him to stay upright. Then he was walking unsteadily towards the hut behind the guards, and watched by a bevy of curious eyes. Margaret found her bare arms rising in goose pimples, and shivered.

She caught his arm as he came in, and hastily undid the cord fastening his wrists. With almost impossible self-control she turned her back on him while searching for the water bottles she had brought across the border with her.

"Why don't you sit down," she invited in a wobbly voice, "and I'll give you a drink."

It was only the wall which was keeping him up, so by the simple expedient of gratefully letting his knees buckle, he slid to the ground and held out a hand for the water. Sweat ran from that fatal red hair, sheening the stubble on his face and soaking into the material of his shirt, but he made no attempt to wipe it away. In fact, he resembled an automaton with no awareness of where he was or what he was doing. Margaret hugged herself tautly as he slowly sipped from the bottle, wasting a lot which splashed on to the mud floor.

Now the moment had come, a ridiculous feeling of faintheartedness prevented her from explaining why he had been set free. An indefinable mind-barrier was preventing any kind of flow between them, and five minutes passed in utter silence until Jan slid sideways and lay on the mat staring at the ceiling.

She took the water-bottle from a hand which was burning! This detachedness must be caused by fever. Over an hour in sunshine which generated a temperature of over a hundred degrees would raise his own to a dangerous level, bringing headaches and vagueness—even temporary blindness, perhaps. A search in her handbag produced aspirin and she went on her knees beside him intending to persuade him to swallow them, but that was as far as she got. One look at his face was enough to convince her that sun-stroke was not wholly responsible for his condition.

"Don't, Jan. It's over now." She put a hand over his eyes to hide what she saw there, and touched her mouth lightly against his.

He turned his head away. "Please, Maggie, the one thing I really *don't* want at this moment is for you to feel you have to make the supreme sacrifice on my behalf."

That was the deciding stroke. The gamble was lost and the jewel would never be a perfect solitaire! In that moment it became clear she had a desperate fight on her hands. This lion had no intention of letting anyone grab him by the mane—especially Margaret Ward! The afternoon blazed into a mellower glory as they lay on their respective mats separated by opposing emotions yet each, with a strange irony, had arrived at a vital turning point.

Jan faced the denouement of his life-long struggle. He had not noticed the black faces surrounding him as he stood in the centre of that compound. The terrible humiliation which had washed over him when the rope had fastened him to the spot had not been caused by these people. They could not be blamed; he knew, only too well, the sway a witch-doctor held with simple tribesmen. It was recollection which had provided the torment. With the slipping on of that collar he had travelled back through the years to a sun-washed prosperous farm where the golden days went on for ever, and nights were purgatory . . . and five children had tied him to a tree.

The Schroeder children had been obsessed with a film concerning a lynch mob, and had consequently decided to re-enact the film the following afternoon. At six years old, Jan had a very small pony, so the others voted that he would have to be the outlaw because their larger mounts would easily outrun his. It had been a wild, hilarious chase with his pony putting up a game fight, but he had soon flagged and the outlaw was captured. They had tied his hands behind him and led him to a tall tree where a noose was slipped over his head. One of his bloodthirsty sisters had pointed out that men sometimes took all day to die if their necks didn't break at the first jerk. Chris had said kindly that Jan's neck, being small, would snap quite easily bringing a quick death. They always went on like that and Jan knew they were joking . . . but there was always that dreadful fear that something would go wrong and it would really happen.

Chris had slung the rope over a branch and was about to lift his youngest brother on to the pony when Kip found a snake, and the capricious enthusiasm of children had found this more diverting than a game which had really gone as far as it could. Chris had killed the creature and they had rushed off to show their father, leaving Jan quite forgotten. He had said the rudest words he knew and prepared to walk the long distance to the house with his hands tied behind him, but only got a few yards before he was pulled up short by the noose round his neck. A knot in the rope had wedged itself between the trunk and the branch and would not pull free.

At first, he didn't realize how helpless he was until attempts to free himself proved useless, but real panic didn't set in until it became obvious the others were not coming back for him. When he became husky from shouting, he tried giving his pony a kick to send it back to the house, but the stupid creature remained loyally by his side. His absence was not noticed until it was time for his supper, and there was all hell to pay!

Randell, who was eighteen and no longer played with the others, his father, with Chris and Kip to guide them to the spot, rode out to bring him home. Jan had never forgotten that scene. The two boys had looked deathly white and frightened for the first time in their lives. Their father had thrashed them both severely and further penalized them by making them work on the farm for the remainder of the school holidays. Chris had gone out of his way to be kind to his small brother after that—

had even offered him the model plane which was his prized possession—but nothing would wipe away the humiliation Jan had felt when the rescue party turned up. He had been crying!

From his earliest days Chris had been his hero. Randell was already grown-up and led his own life, George, his nearest brother, was a book-worm, the girls didn't count, but Chris, nine years older, was perfect! It was Chris who thought of all the daring escapades; Chris who found the haunted *kopje* first, who drove the tractor without Father's knowledge, who brewed home-made beer in his bedroom. Chris was tall, fearless, and infallible in the eyes of the young Jan. The one big snag was Kip! Only eleven months separated the spiritual twins so it was Kip who commanded Chris's brotherly affection, sharing all his secrets and confidences. They also shared a bedroom, which made Jan burn with resentment, and he was often found curled up on Chris's bed when the older boys went up and had to be carried back to the room known as the nursery.

When Chris became an airline pilot, Jan was filled with envy and vowed he would be a flier, too . . . but it was Kip who was asked to be a partner in Schroeder Freight at the birth of the company. For the first time, the brothers had variant ideas and Kip stuck to his desire to be a farmer like their father. Jan seized his chance and took an apprenticeship in aircraft maintenance, at Chris's suggestion. Even that didn't bring him any closer to his hero; it was still Kip who claimed that honour. He even stole one of his brother's girl-friends and married her, but Chris had met Helen by then and didn't hold it against Kip.

Eventually, the chance came for Jan to learn to fly and he applied himself eagerly. He acquired the licence in record time which earned lavish praise from Chris, yet his request for another aircraft which was unanimously turned down by the rest of the family seemed remarkably like a vote of no-confidence in his ability. When Chris accepted the decision without question it put the seal on twenty years of imagined inadequacy, and started him on the road which had ended with another rope round his neck.

The bitter taste of failure was still in his mouth as he lay on the floor of the primitive hut that afternoon. As a child, his elaborate efforts to impress Chris had been unsuccessful; more recently, his subconscious continuation of the theme had resulted in complete disaster. The lunatic urge to become a second Chris had driven him to a way of life he didn't enjoy among people he had no respect for. Now, the final unacceptable blow! Van Heerdon's words out there under the sun filled him with disgust. If one man thought him capable of selling his brother out and embarking on large-scale crime, how many more held the same opinion? Did Chris himself?

He threw an arm up over his eyes in an attempt to blot out the mental images which flogged at his brain, and the sweat flowed freely as he rode out his anger during the long hot afternoon, but when the hands of his watch stood at four-thirty, he was calm and resolute enough to let himself sleep. His next awakening would be metamorphic as well as physical!

As he slept, Margaret watched him, knowing such scrutiny would be out of the question when he was awake. The camera of her new love photographed every detail so that the pictures could be brought out in some future winter to recapture the spring of this moment. Throughout the afternoon she had seen his restlessness, had known he was living through some personal agony of mind which his make-up prevented him from sharing with her, but his brow was unfurrowed and his hands were relaxed in sleep. His quality of complete independence, although it hurt her, nevertheless earned her admiration. She traced the stubborn set of his mouth and the strength of a jaw which had clamped tightly shut on the excuses he could have produced to offset the anger his actions had induced in another; the red-gold lashes lying against the shadows beneath his eyes; a small white scar behind one ear which was probably the result of some childish escapade. All these things increased her awareness of him, telling her that from now on his every look, every touch, would be like striking a match in the parched *veld*.

She decided to wake him at five-thirty. The sun was dipping very low and Van Heerdon would be back for his answer once the light had gone. As before, Jan slept like the dead. Margaret ended up slapping his face when pokes and prods had no effect, but even then he came to the surface in slow motion.

"Oooh! I guessed it was you when those matron-like slaps rained on me. Any other woman would have woken me gently."

She smiled her delight at his return to normal. "I've tried that method. It doesn't work half as quickly as a slap!"

"I don't know why you couldn't let me sleep in peace," he grumbled. "It's not as if there were anything to wake up for."

"Van Heerdon is coming back at sunset."

"Is he!" That brought him instantly alert. "In that case I must talk to you quickly."

"I want to talk to *you*," she put in.

"Whatever it is can be said later. This is urgent. Now listen carefully and don't interrupt!" He sat up and put his hand on her arm, little knowing what the contact did to her. "It appears my flying skill is a valuable commodity to Van Heerdon . . . so valuable he has made me a very attractive proposition. At first, I told him what to do with it, but I've weighed up the alternatives and decided to accept."

"I see," she said with a frozen face.

"It's *your* position I'm worried about. Whatever idiocy persuaded you to follow me this morning has led you into a situation I wouldn't wish on anyone . . . even you! This isn't Norfolk, you know. Here, you are dealing with the native mind, which is something no white man will ever completely understand, and to these people women are in the lower order. Their function is simply to carry the burdens, till the fields, harvest the crops, cook the food . . . and bear the sons! They are not expected to have any finer feelings and their worth is based on their stamina. As far as you are concerned, you didn't even rate an evil spell from the witch-doctor—you are nothing!"

"Thanks, that's done my ego no end of good."

It made him angry. "This is no time for flippancy, Maggie. Your only chance to live is if I take you with me, and God knows that's the last thing I want to do. When Van Heerdon comes back let me do all the talking, and for once in your life, do as you are told! Can I have your word on that?"

There was nothing she wanted more than for him to take charge of everything. Since

258

his startling announcement, a strange limbo of mind and body had overtaken her, leaving her with the desire to think of nothing more perplexing than how she could have a wash and change into fresh clothes.

Van Heerdon might be a self-confessed soul of generosity when it came to payment of his employees, but he was a miser with time. The sun had still not completely disappeared when Margaret, at the window aperture, saw him crossing the compound. Apart from telling Jan of his coming, she kept silent during the short proceedings, and Van Heerdon showed no surprise at Jan's acceptance of his offer. Even when the pilot made the proviso that Margaret should accompany them, he merely nodded and said, "Naturally."

Things moved quickly after that, although the night had moved even quicker. The brief dusk had changed into darkness by the time they left the hut and were conducted across to the stockade.

"I fear you will have to avoid this *kraal* from now on, Jan. Having been told that you are bad medicine these people will be dedicated for life to killing you if you ever appear here unshackled. They hunt over quite a large area, so bear that in mind, won't you," said Van Heerdon by way of a gentle warning against possible treachery. "Have you ever seen the results of a medicine murder?" he asked, and went on to describe in detail some of the cases in recent years during the drive in the jeep which had been waiting for them outside the *kraal*.

It was impossible to follow the route. Sitting beside the black driver Margaret was only aware of ghost trees which loomed at them in the lights from their headlamps as they bounced and zig-zagged over the rough track. Apart from that island of light, the rest of the night was dark, humid and alien. She was reminded of that other nocturnal journey in the police truck with Jan driving like a demon, and yet another before that with him stretched at her feet, dazed with pain. Her nights in Africa were doomed to be spent in careering about the countryside, it seemed.

When the cessation of movement brought her suddenly awake Margaret thought they had gone round in a circle. The *kraal* looked exactly like the one they had left, but her illusion was soon dismissed when she saw the inhabitants. Certainly the women wore the same wrap-around skirts and bead belts which left their breasts bare, and their fuzzy hair was built into similar gigantic beehives, but the men were vastly different from the warriors she had seen leaping round Jan. These were in loose-fitting camouflage uniforms, floppy jungle-green hats, and jungle boots. Most of them lounged around in doorways, but several were posted at vantage points around the stockade and carried rifles. They looked unreal, like extras on a film set, until Margaret realized Van Heerdon had brought them to the rebel head-quarters.

9

THEY got out and the jeep shot off into a makeshift garage formed by camouflage nets strung between trees, then Van Heerdon led them behind the grass-topped huts on to a well-worn path running uphill away from the *kraal*. They must have walked for a good ten minutes before the way became rocky and uneven, slowing their progress and making the two men breathe heavily: Van Heerdon because of a thickening waistline, Jan because of his exhausted condition.

At last, after a further five minutes of climbing, the beam from Van Heerdon's torch hit a wall of rock and revealed a cleft wide enough to admit a man's body. It shouldn't have come as a surprise to see Craig Barker sitting there on an upturned box, but this definite proof of his villainy shook Margaret. He did not look as debonair as at Myala. The gauche bravado he assumed was not given any credence by the twitching of a nerve at the corner of his mouth when he saw who had entered.

"Ha!" he exclaimed a trifle overloudly. "I thought you'd sing a different song when it became a choice between your skin and that of your precious brother. Admit it, Jan, underneath we are *all* devoted to self-preservation." When Jan failed to answer he raised his arms, then let them fall. "Sorry about that affair this morning, but you do see that I hadn't any choice? No hard feelings,eh?"

"No hard feelings," repeated Jan amicably, "but when I find you without two assistants to hold my arms, we'll have a return match."

"My, my, the spirit of fire still burns despite the ordeal by rope. You do realize that is the method they use to tether their scrawny goats!"

"Yes, and they let the vermin run loose."

Van Heerdon had had enough of this and put an end to it by indicating one of the beds and telling Margaret she could sleep there. "It's a trifle primitive, I fear, but food will be sent up from one of the women before long, and there is plenty of water. I regret the need to stay here tonight, but the man I have come to see is away on a mission with a small explosives party and won't be back until tomorrow. Because of that, he is not yet aware of the slight problem we have run up against. I also want to make sure he deals with the men who were insane enough to kill Russell Martin and leave the body as proof of the act. The authorities are well aware which tribe uses that method on murder victims, and there is bound to be a fever of checking at the various *kraals* in the vicinity.

He lowered himself on to the other bed and sighed. "It's always the same where they are concerned. A perfectly organized operation is endangered by a lightning reversal to tribal custom. It's the one thing which keeps them from supremacy in this country."

While he was speaking, Margaret put her bag and the water bottles on the bed and looked around. The cave she was in was virtually a rocky arsenal housing the supplies of weapons and ammunition which Jan and other willing or innocent men had delivered to this part of Africa. Aside from the camp beds, several paraffin tins filled with water were lined along one side with earthenware bowls instead of cups, and upturned crates beside a small fissure provided a seat for look-out men. Margaret was no expert on military supplies, but there seemed to be enough to keep a large force well armed.

The meal was some sort of stew which, despite its heavy flavour, suggested it might be better not to ask its ingredients. Margaret ate it all. Apart from the cheese and apples, she had had nothing since the previous evening and had reached the stage where hunger overcame caution. Without making it obvious she noted Jan had emptied his bowl, had it re-filled, and was rapidly making the second helping vanish. That was good; another sign of the return to complete normality. Deeming it prudent to remain in the background, she had ample time to study the men as they talked and it struck her that Jan was containing some sort of volcanic emotion beneath his quiet interest. That he was interested was beyond doubt, for the questions he asked were pertinent and razor-sharp enough to bring a gleam of triumph to Van Heerdon's eyes.

What they were planning was frightening! Chris was to be disposed of by a masterly combination of under-selling and business espionage which would leave him with the alternative of accepting Jan's take-over, or bankrupting himself. Once Schroeder Freight was in Jan's hands, Van Heerdon would staff it with trusted men, and provide aircraft which had a longer range. They planned to go international as soon as possible. At this point it struck Margaret that Schroeder Freight might be run by the two brothers, but it was owned by the entire family. Helen had told her each male member held shares so that any profits or losses were distributed among them . . . and hadn't she also said the family usually outvoted Jan? How, then, could he sit there planning a future with Van Heerdon when he knew it was not a simple matter of getting rid of Chris to set them on the road to success?

Van Heerdon had only recently broken into the gun-running business and was in danger of losing the contract from the American firm which supplied them because he had been unable to feed enough markets. As it was, he had a warehouse full of surplus weapons just waiting to be shipped out the minute Jan was ready. The buyers were there just begging for the chance to get their hands on the weapons, but Van Heerdon was no fool. Until he had a watertight set-up he was not going to risk being caught, even if it meant losing the contract. Maybe events had proved advantageous, after all. They had brought matters to a head and forced a decision from all concerned.

"I don't yet see what part I am to play in this organization," put in Craig. "Since I can't go back to Myala, you must have something planned for me."

Van Heerdon put down his bowl and stretched. "I have, don't worry! It will be essential to get you out of the country and it so happens I know of just the place. One of my future customers in the Suez area will find your services invaluable. Your job at Myala educated you somewhat in the clerical arts, I should imagine."

Craig darkened angrily. "Now look, I am a university graduate in animal sciences, not a bloody little clerk."

"I know, dear boy, but when you chose to panic and run last night you forfeited any claim to continue your profession. Had you kept a clear head you might be there yet."

"It's easy for you to say that! There's never any risk attached to the part *you* play, sitting there like a fat spider in the centre of a web. You don't know what I've been through these past three days. When I heard Jan had come down in the *veld* it was a severe shock coming on top of Russell Martin's discovery of the poaching, believe me. Then, when the Rangers turned up with that hideous corpse, it put the fear of God into me. I understood they were bringing him here to Mtubu as a prisoner, or I would never have let them take him over the border. It wasn't necessary to kill him in that vile manner."

His voice had risen slightly and Margaret recognized the signs of subdued hysteria in the young man. He was reaching the end of his tether and turned on Jan as an escape route for his anger. "If you hadn't put on such a heavy act of brotherly outrage and shown your true colours, none of this would have happened." He turned back to Van Heerdon. "What would you have done when Jan burst in driving a stolen police truck which would set the law hot on his trail?"

"I should have joined forces with him instead of putting his back up. He needs special handling."

"Please stop analysing me as if I were not here," put in Jan.

"Yes," sneered Craig, ignoring him, "and what would you have done about *her*!" He nodded towards Margaret.

"*You* ask *me*!" jibed Van Heerdon, bringing another flush to the young man's face. "It is perfectly plain you lose *all* your senses when in a tight corner . . . that's why the office job will suit you admirably."

Craig stood up, unable to control himself. "I won't do it!"

"Then stay here and be charged with the murder of Russell Martin."

The ruddy colour drained from his face, leaving him looking like a living corpse in the harsh light from the paraffin lamps.

"But I didn't kill him!"

"Your flight from Myala will convince the police that you did. Coming on top of the recovery of the body, it will condemn you without a trial."

"They have no witnesses, no proof. I'll deny it."

"And what reason will you give for beating up a pilot (the Rangers witnessed that, don't forget) and disappearing into the night with two accomplices? Don't you think the penalty for gun-running will be as severe, when added to the charge of illegal poaching?"

"What about *them*?" he asked wildly. "Him and his *flerric*. What makes you think *they* can continue working in this country?"

"They will earn all praise for their courageous pursuit of a desperate killer. Unfortunately, you slipped through their fingers across the border and vanished to an unknown destination. You do see you have no choice?"

Craig stood for a moment, rocking slightly and clenching his fists in an empty threat, but contrary to Margaret's assessment the breaking point had not yet been reached, and he muttered, "You've got everything neatly slotted, haven't you?" before slumping on to the crates by the fissure and gazing into the night.

The atmosphere calmed somewhat after

270

that small crisis and Margaret felt tiredness creeping through her limbs like a gentle tide benignly but implacably claiming the shore. The soft conversation between Jan and Van Heerdon provided a lulling background, and she was only half-awake when two uniformed men arrived to take over from the ones who had stood guard during the earlier part of the evening. When Van Heerdon had expressed a hope that she might not find the bed too uncomfortable, Jan had put in, "It's all right. She likes Spartan conditions," but she was not as tough as he imagined. Despite her exhausted state her night was spent like a jack-in-the-box, leaping up from the depths one minute, then sinking back to the darkness of sleep the next. The waking periods seemed spaced approximately an hour apart, she noted with interest; each time she roused, the hands of her watch had moved on to the next figure on the luminous dial.

The second time she turned restlessly and opened her eyes, she saw Jan lying alongside her bed on a couple of blankets spread upon the ground. Only one paraffin lamp was left alight, casting an eerie glow over the sleeping figures—sleeping, that is, except for herself and the man beside her. He lay on his back smoking a cigarette and gazing at the ceiling. With all her senses she willed him to look her way, but they were not even on the same wave-length.

Jan was off in the realms of his solitary thought processes which meant he was unaware of anybody, but this time Margaret felt a sharp envy of whatever was occupying his mind and was reminded again of the impossible goal she was aiming for. She could be grateful for only one thing. Whatever Jan was planning, he would ensure her safety . . . but that would be the end of their association! Somehow she had to contrive a way of keeping in constant touch with him even if it meant artful cultivation of her friendship with Helen Schroeder. With matters so desperate she would push aside her scruples and use every means at her disposal. But this affair was by no means over. Jan was playing a dangerous game at the moment and many things might happen before it was resolved. For all she knew, her wooing of the man she wanted might have to take place through prison bars!

Towards morning, Margaret's hourly break in sleep brought her eyes open to find Craig Barker lying on his side watching her as he smoked a cigarette with nervous dedication. Her instinctive shrugging further beneath the blanket brought a twist to his mouth. A remembrance of how he had compensated for the smaller humiliation Jan had meted out in her presence sent apprehension to weaken her limbs. A known womanizer would not take easily to the defeat he had suffered at Van Heerdon's hands which had undermined his male superiority in front of the only female present. His continued scrutiny had her thanking providence for Jan's six feet two of hard muscle between them, even though she knew from experience that his present sleep would probably continue through fire, flood, and any number of rapacious attacks on her person. She found it impossible to relax again, knowing Craig's state of mind, and the guards were replaced at dawn with no further sleep having come to her.

Never had she dreaded the onset of a new day, but this one threatened to be fraught with danger. Although Van

Heerdon appeared to have no suspicion that Jan was not with him one hundred per cent, it only needed one small slip to enlighten him. So far, Jan had been coldly clever, but once that temper of his was roused it would be a different matter. One possible irritant, herself, could be ruled out because she intended remaining quietly in the background, but Craig Barker was a different proposition. He had already baited Jan with sneering remarks and if things were destined to go wrong, *he* would be the cause. She sighed. The most lethal weapons in this arsenal were human!

The first set-back came when Mtubu, the guerrilla leader, failed to turn up when expected. Van Heerdon became tetchy which didn't help the general mood amongst the group of white people isolated in the rocks, and after several hours of waiting he decided to go down to the *kraal* to investigate.

"No doubt a message has come through and those bloody kaffirs are too lazy to climb up here to give it to me," he fumed. "I can't afford to kick my heels in this back-block of Africa. Time means rands to me, but they don't think of that. In fact, they just don't *think*! That's half their trouble."

Margaret dearly wished to comment on why he continued to trade with people he so obviously despised, but gamely stuck to her resolution to stay in the background. She succeeded so well Jan was moved to ask if she were feeling all right, and when she assured him she was, added: "Never known you lost for words before. Dare I hope it heralds a new era?"

"Yes, if it makes you happy," she said with a smile and received a rare one in return which unsettled her even more.

Craig had gone outside some minutes before, and Jan left also, stating that he wanted to have a look around the place in daylight. Since the two guards were lounging outside in the sunshine, it gave Margaret the perfect opportunity to wash herself in privacy. She stripped off her torn blouse and splashed herself liberally with water from the tins along the wall. It was heavenly to feel fresh and clean once more. She completed the job by smoothing cologne from her bag over her arms and throat. It reminded her of tangy ferns back in Norfolk.

A slight sound which echoed in the high-vaulted chamber sent her spinning round. Craig stood there grinning with her blouse in his hand.

"Very nice! I always like my women on the generous side," he mused as he ran his eyes over the curve of her breasts showing above the pale lace. "The whiteness of your skin is exciting after the sun-tanned South African girls."

"If that is meant as a compliment, thank you," she said. "Now I'll have my blouse back."

"Come and get it," he invited with luminous eyes.

"Oh, grow up! In England boys of sixteen have discarded that trick."

Incensed, Craig muttered, "You are not in England now. I'll show you some tricks they've never even heard of over there." He advanced towards her, dropping the blouse on the floor.

Margaret retreated instinctively, knowing the method she had used to discourage Jan would not work in this instance. At the same time she acknowledged that never, at any time, had she been afraid of *him* as she was of this man now.

The problem was desperate. If she called out, it might bring Jan running and spark off the very situation she was trying so hard to avoid, but her chances of getting away from Craig were practically nil. To keep going backwards would spell disaster for the cave narrowed into nothingness, so her only chance was to fool him somehow and make a dash for it. No bright ideas occurred to her. With Jan her wits had been sharpened by his, but her brain was in a hiatus for this dilemma.

Craig had reached her and stood close, smiling down as one hand started to caress her arm.

"If we had worked together at Myala there would have been time for some titil-lating scuffles before we came to grips, but things have changed in the last twenty-four hours and I want you without any feminine provocation first."

Like lightning, his arms were round her and his hands fumbled with the fastening of her lacy bra while fleshy lips sucked at her mouth with messy ardour. She struggled, then cursed her stupidity when his arms clamped tighter round her. Hadn't she told Jan she knew the consequences of a woman fighting off an embrace? She felt the straps slipping from her shoulders, and since he had her arms pinned to her sides, used her feet. Without shoes on, his shins suffered very little; in fact, the attack only spurred him on. He lifted his mouth and laughed in triumphant breathlessness.

"Ha! Got you rattled at last, have I? I've been watching you and wondering what it would take to shake that touch-me-not air you assume. I passed my waking hours last night imagining this moment, and it is every bit as exciting as I thought it would be." He ran his tongue along her lips. "I want you because you make a man fight for what he gets. I also want you because you are the sexiest thing I have seen around for four months . . . but the most supreme satisfaction I shall get out of taking you is knowing you belong to Jan. There is no more exquisite delight than telling a man you dislike that you have just bedded his woman."

Margaret seized at this straw and gasped, "I'm not his woman . . . or ever likely to be. He can't wait to get shot of me at the first opportunity."

"Yes?" sneered Craig. "Then why did he bring you with him from Myala?"

"He didn't. I followed him. He doesn't care a fig about me."

"Let's test that theory, shall we." Craig's second kiss was worse than the first, and Margaret was revolted by the wet lips, the rasp of stubble against her cheek, and the smell of stale sweat. She was being slowly forced backwards when an almighty explosion slammed against their ears, jerking them apart and bringing a string of oaths from the man beside her.

"The next one will be aimed *at* you," said Van Heerdon, still pointing the revolver in their direction. "You disgust me with your uncontrollable mating instincts, especially at a time like this." He walked towards them. "I am *not* having this venture marred by the human version of the rutting season! Now, get down to the *kraal* and find out what those bastards are muttering about. I can't get any sense out of them, but you know the language and should have no difficulty in discovering what all their frenzied activity is for."

Craig stumbled past the armed man without a word while Margaret tried to control her shivering as she retrieved her blouse and dressed herself. Van Heerdon ignored her and left the cave on Craig's heels for which she was thankful, but her shivering was not entirely due to the fright she had received at the hands of the Assistant Warden. When sane thought returned it was to bring the question of how long Van Heerdon had been watching the scene. Had he heard her deny being Jan's mistress . . . admit that Jan would rid himself of her at the first opportunity? If so, she was in jeopardy!

As morning dragged into afternoon Margaret relaxed. Van Heerdon gave no sign that he distrusted her, although it was anything but quiet amongst the group waiting there. Craig discovered from the inhabitants of the *kraal* that one of the high days of the tribe was a festival held on this particular day (the nineteenth of December on the European calendar) and this year was to be no exception. Guerrilla tactics, stolen arms, the fight against oppression . . . all were laid aside while rejoicing and celebrations took place. Van Heerdon raged, but there was nothing he could do. Men cast off their camouflage uniforms and dressed in their finery for the occasion. The women happily prepared batches of cakes and spicy meatballs which would be among the delicacies washed down by the home-brewed beer forming the basis of these tribal festivals.

Margaret came across Jan on the outskirts of the *kraal* where he watched the preparations while he smoked a cigarette beneath the shade of some trees. Her words of greeting startled him from a reverie, but when she asked only interested questions about life in a *kraal* he relaxed and answered to the best of his ability. No mention was made of things now past, and they chatted companionably with no indication that they were anything other than tourists to this part of Africa. She loved listening to his strangely accented words as he told her all he knew about native customs and lore. It could not be termed extensive knowledge, but it was recounted with such sincerity that Margaret found herself drawn to him even more.

Already the comings and goings between huts had doubled, and Jan said there were probably neighbours and friends from other *kraals* visiting them for the evening highlights. The rough stalls containing sweetmeats were continously surrounded, and the *kaffirbier* was flowing freely. There seemed to be an endless supply of it and Jan gave his opinion that they would all be "sloshed" by morning. "It's not your sort of evening," he said with a smile which knocked her sideways. She marvelled at his recent addiction to smiling. He had never walked on thinner ice yet there was a calmness and sense of peace which had never been there before.

Around late afternoon, Mtubu, the guerrilla leader, arrived back, and Van Heerdon sent Craig to demand Jan's immediate presence.

"He only wants *you*," said Craig pointedly and ambled off again.

"Mmm," said Jan, looking after his retreating figure, "that fellow is very quiet today. Do you suppose Van Heerdon has been at him again?"

"I have no idea," lied Margaret. "Perhaps he's not feeling well."

"Maybe." He started to walk off.

"Jan."

"Yes?"

"You are not really going through with this, are you?"

"Yes." The barrier was back bearing the NO ENTRY sign.

The day went from bad to worse after that, with Van Heerdon's temper being severely strained and personalities beginning to clash. Mtubu had been delighted with the new plans, but regretted that nothing could be done about their departure until the following day. Indeed, he suggested it was far safer for the whole group to stay up in the arsenal until the celebrations were over because Mtubu couldn't answer for what his people might do when the drink possessed them. It was not unknown for violence to break out during the latter stages of these affairs when old or imagined grievances were dragged to the fore on a tide of *bier*, and the following morning produced a flotsam of casualties. Mtubu made no secret of the fact that he was anxious to get out his festival outfit and join in the laughter and dancing himself.

Van Heerdon sat moodily on his bed disinclined to speak, Craig was still absent —watching the bare bosoms of the dancing girls, Margaret guessed cynically—and Jan

283

lay on his blanket smoking yet another cigarette. Margaret had occupied ten minutes by inspecting the stitches in Jan's thigh and re-covering the tender flesh with a large dressing from the medical equipment available there. After that, she found time hanging heavily. It was an oppressive evening and the drums beating down in the *kraal* were beginning to bring back dreadful memories.

An hour later, she could stand it no longer and stood up to leave the confines of the cave before she made a fool of herself.

"Where are you going?" asked Jan sharply.

"I have to get some air. I won't go far."

Van Heerdon made no attempt to stop her but watched her departure with a new gleam in his eye. It was possible to look down on the compound from a vantage point a few yards down the path, so Margaret made for the spot and leant back against a tree with a sigh. Out here in the vast night her fears receded and the drumming bothered her less. Soon, she became interested in the ritual below, which was as colourful and bizarre as anything she had ever seen. The women were dancing one behind the other in a long, long snake which undulated around the outside of the compound to the accompaniment of weird chanting and stamping of feet. At the same time, their menfolk, decked out with feathers and brief bead skirts, performed a maniacal dance in the centre. Their stamina was astounding! They had been at it since early evening and Margaret's watch showed past midnight with no sign of their tiring. When the dancers needed refreshment they drank as they went, and the steps became noticeably more frenzied after each draught.

The whole affair was becoming compulsive viewing. By the light of the many flaming torches the glistening black bodies in their vivid costumes bettered any spectacular produced at the West End, and the rhythmic beat of drum and feet brought a primitive response from any listener within range. Once again Margaret recognized the hypnotic power of this type of ceremonial. The night was filled with throbbing sounds which thrilled yet scared her, such was the design of that tribal music which grew louder and louder as the participants grew more frenzied.

Suddenly, all music ceased with a silence louder than an explosive bang, and into the compound leapt the grotesque bird-figure of yesterday. Margaret gasped and drew back instinctively at the sight of the witch-doctor. A quick desire for company sent her hurrying back up the path, but just outside the cave a black figure loomed out of the darkness with hands outstretched. Her scream stopped him in his tracks, but even as Jan appeared through the opening in the wall of rock, Margaret recognized the man as one of the guards the previous evening and apologized for her reaction. Her words brought forth an indication that he understood that she hadn't recognized him in his feathers. He had brought some *bier* and cakes for his white guests.

"Hey!" called a voice from above, and Craig dropped to the ground from his seat on the rocks above the cave's entrance. "Count me in on this. You get a fantastic view of the compound from up there," he explained of his sudden appearance. "Why don't you come up?"

"Maybe I will," said Jan in view of Craig's sudden affability. "It's impossible to sleep through this row."

The black man took decorated containers from the top of the jug and poured the brew into the first one, which he gave to Jan. Jan passed it to Margaret automatically, but that didn't please their host. He took it from her hands with a slight shake of his head and gave it back to Jan. It was men first according to his upbringing. Women had what was left over! Craig was served next, then Margaret. Jan quickly advised her not to refuse unless she wished to offend the man, so used to this at parties, she made a pretence at sipping until such time as she could tip it away. When the man had gone, Craig soon put a stop to what she had planned.

"It's criminal to pour that stuff away," he said, taking it from her. "*You* may need to keep your wits about you with three men breathing down your neck, but *I* plan to whoop it up tonight—and may the best man win!"

That was a challenge which Jan chose to ignore as he slowly drank from his coloured pot. In the end, Margaret climbed on the rocks with the two men with some vague thought of acting as mediator should it be necessary, and also because it was a better alternative to staying in the cave where Jan said Van Heerdon was snoring loudly. Sitting up there looking into the clearing was rather like being on the business end of a spotlight operated from the gallery of a theatre, and as such, made the scene less real. With Jan beside her she felt no sinister fears of the bird-like witch-doctor, and even began to regard the whole thing as a musical extravaganza.

Craig's earlier chatter had lessened until he seemed to be as engrossed in it as the other two, so when his hand suddenly grabbed her arm it made Margaret jump.

"What . . . Craig, what's the matter?" she asked when she turned and saw his face in the moonlight. It looked grotesque, a mask like those being worn by the Africans down in the *kraal*, with twisted features and bulging eyes.

His fingers dug into her flesh until she gasped with the pain of it, but what she was watching caused more pain. The once burly young man had grown aged and withered within minutes and his mouth was stretched back in a mirthless grin.

"Jan!" she cried in a strangled voice. "Look at him! Oh dear God, look at him!"

There was no time to do anything. Before their horrified eyes Craig Barker twisted into a tortured position and, without uttering a sound, died of his agony ten seconds later.

10

MARGARET sat with her face buried in Jan's shoulder unwilling to believe the evidence of her own eyes. She had seen enough pets innocently killed by eating rat poison or gardening products to recognize the cause of Craig's death, but the passing regret she felt for a small furry creature's agony was nothing to the revulsion she experienced now. Death should be clean and dignified—anything which desecrated or maimed brought a crawling, choking sickness to her stomach. Craig Barker was an unlikeable lecher, but his body had been strong and young and attractive. It should never have become the unspeakable thing it was now!

Jan seemed equally frozen with shock. They must have sat welded together for some time before either of them was able to think clearly. When they did, there was one conclusion they both reached without difficulty.

"I had a feeling Craig would never reach

Suez, but I didn't think Van Heerdon would act so quickly. I would have tried to save him, you know."

Margaret nodded against him, her heart leaden.

"Why did he do it now . . . why?" continued Jan emphatically. "There was no reason."

"Yes, there was. I killed him as surely as if I had administered the stuff myself." She pulled away from him. "It was my presence here which hastened his death."

"I think you had better explain that remark." His voice was low and controlled, but there was a bite in it, nevertheless. "The time has come for you to put your cards on the table, Maggie. Just why did you follow me here instead of returning to headquarters, and why does Van Heerdon accept your presence so readily? There was nothing going on between you and Craig, was there? You didn't arrange with him to wake me up that night so that he could give me a good hiding before he left? You made a pretty convincing effort to try to stop me following him."

"That's unforgivable!"

"Is it?"

The pause went on long enough for the moment to cool a little then Margaret admitted, "I should have been completely honest before now, but there was no reason for you to say what you did. I had only known Craig for a few hours when he left Myala. He may have been a womanizer, but I don't fall under the spell that quickly . . . as you should know!"

"I'm sorry. Perhaps I was subconsciously confronting you with your own tactics. You have accused *me* of some pretty low tricks."

"Yes," was all she would trust herself to say. "But it's too late for quarrelling, Jan. I'm frightened." She dug her fingers into the thick hair laying heavily against her scalp. "How do you think the poison was given to him?"

"Not in the supper tonight—we all served ourselves from the same container. It must have been in the beer . . . at least, not in the *beer* but the pot he drank from. These tribal chiefs and witch-doctors are dab hands at poisons. It would be easy to put a little powder in the base of one of those drinking pots."

"*Two* of the drinking pots," she corrected.

"Eh?"

"If you remember, the first cup was given to you, but when you passed it to me in a rush of good manners, it was firmly given back to you because it was the only one which was safe to drink from."

"But that's . . ."

"You are the only person who knew I never take intoxicants, and when Craig gaily grabbed mine from me he was condemning himself to an agonizing death by swallowing twice the dose. I can't swear to the ingredients of the poison, but a single dose would have probably ensured death some time during the night by a slow paralysis of the body which would leave him looking fairly normal by morning—would leave *us* looking fairly normal, I should say. One of my long list of virtues saved my life!"

Jan grabbed her arm. "Maggie, you had better tell me why Van Heerdon suddenly wants you out of the way. If I am to get us away from here, I have to know everything."

"I think that goes for both of us. I admit

I really believed you had accepted Van Heerdon's terms until I heard you discussing details with him. Jan, you *know* it isn't just a case of ousting Chris from Schroeder Freight. Your whole family has shares in it—Helen told me. Yet you have agreed to all Van Heerdon suggested. How long are you hoping to fool him?"

He didn't answer the question. "Leave *me* to do all the worrying and tell me why he wants you out of the way."

There was no alternative but to make a clean breast of everything.

"I'm not as cold-blooded as you imagine, and the sight of you tied up in that compound while the people went about their daily routine was more than I could bear. I have seen unspeakable things done to animals, but I didn't realize how I would feel when I saw a human suffering from a deliberate act of inhumanity. Van Heerdon was prepared to leave you there until you were on your knees, but I told him I could persuade you to change your mind if he cut you loose and left us alone for a while He gave me until sundown, but you took the decision yourself, not knowing it would strengthen his belief that I was your mistress. My apparent success must have persuaded him that you were deeply entangled with me and therefore I would be a useful ally in the future."

"Go on."

"This morning I made a stupid mistake. The inevitable happened and I lost my head. Craig said it would delight him to take your girl while your back was turned, and in the heat of the moment, I denied everything . . . said you couldn't wait to see the last of me. Van Heerdon broke it up at that point. He humiliated Craig even further, and although he acted as though I were not there, I was afraid of how much he had heard before he stopped the attempted rape. An influential mistress for his star employee was one thing; an unwanted girl who knew too much was another. So there is your answer. I was too big a risk, and Craig was too big a nuisance!"

"Why didn't you tell me of our supposed relationship? I could have given the game away at any time."

"I didn't think it likely. You were being very careful to play it Van Heerdon's way." She took a deep breath. "Apart from that, I didn't want you to know it was I who gained your release; that I had been fighting your battles for you again."

"I see. Is that why you followed me across the border . . . to fight my battles?"

"Not really," she lied. "I was scared of losing myself in that vast place. I meant it when I said I was hopeless at navigation."

"I offered to get a Ranger out to steer you back."

"I couldn't let you get in touch with headquarters."

"Why not?"

"You are not going to like what I tell you."

"That won't be unusual!"

"When I spoke to Chris on the radio-telephone he told me he intended flying up to Myala to take us back to Cape Town yesterday morning. Caught on the wrong foot, I pretended I couldn't hear what he said and rang off. It seemed wiser not to say anything to you."

His temper, which had been carefully damped down recently, blazed up again at that news, making Margaret realize that putting her cards on the table didn't mean she couldn't have kept back the ace of spades. Jan left her in no doubt that he would have talked Chris out of making the journey had he known and stopped his brother from getting involved in any of this. Now, it was too late! Chris would have set all kinds of wheels in motion, making it pointless for Jan to continue his masquerade with Van Heerdon.

"The police will be on to this already, so my chances of getting Chris off the hook are nil," he said bitterly. "I intended playing along until I had had time to obliterate any evidence that Chris had taken supplies to Myala in recent months. Then I was going to let the organization make their first move towards pushing Chris out of Schroeder Freight, and *that* would have clinched his innocence well and truly. However, as I once told you, my brothers are all very honest and upright, so the minute Chris arrives at Myala to find everyone gone and a dead Warden in the storehouse, he will contact all the correct authorities, little knowing what they will uncover. He will be turning the key in his own prison cell!"

Margaret sat for several seconds while her spirits reached rock-bottom. "I'm so sorry."

"It's too late to be sorry. Just never come back to Africa once you leave!"

That remark hit her badly. Apart from its emotional implications it raised the awful doubt of being allowed to leave anywhere ever again. But for her teetotal habit, she would be in the hands of death now. Surely, her present safety was simply a postponement of the inevitable! Real paralysing fright beset her, casting aside all other considerations.

"You won't have to worry about my future," she cried. "He'll never let me go. You must see that!"

He took her arm and shook her. "Stop it! You are getting overdramatic. Why pick this moment to go all womanly? If ever I needed your cool, competent personality, it's now. Don't let me down!"

He could not have known those last words would act like a charm—tact and insight were hardly strong points in his make-up—but she responded immediately.

"I don't see that there is anything I can do, but you know I'll help you if I can."

"Thanks. We have to get back to Myala right away. I had hoped to give the police a tip which would allow them to move in and catch Van Heerdon red-handed. However, I have most of the information already, and although they may run the minute they know we have escaped, the law will catch up with them eventually. We can give them the arch villain, if nothing else."

"You're crazy, Jan. How can we get away when we are surrounded by rebel guerrillas? Van Heerdon would give the alarm the minute he found us gone."

"We have the perfect opportunity *now*. The natives are all drunk, and we shall take Van Heerdon with us. There's no problem."

He made it sound so easy, but when Margaret heard what he was proposing to do she renewed her conclusion that he was crazy. They climbed down from the rocks, trying not to kick loose pieces which would advertise their presence. It was not easy in the moonlight, and Margaret had to concentrate very hard to keep her mind off Craig's body which remained lodged above them. Once they reached the ground, Jan flung his arm round her shoulders and whispered, "Right. Off we go!"

Van Heerdon was not really sleeping, as Jan had guessed, and his eyes shot open at their entry. The tremor in Margaret's voice did not have to be affected, it was real enough, when she said what Jan had told her to say.

"He has been taken ill. It must have been that native beer. He drank mine as well as his own, and it seems to have upset him badly."

Jan's groans as he staggered beside her were so realistic Van Heerdon's face turned ashen. "What!" he gasped out as he struggled from the bed.

Margaret lowered Jan on to the one she had used and, true to expectation, Van Heerdon crossed the floor to bend over him before turning a vindictive face towards the girl.

"You've killed him, you little bi . . ." He got no further because Jan brought his hands up to take Van Heerdon's throat in a choking grip, and Margaret quickly took the revolver from his belt. Within minutes, Jan had his prisoner's hands tied behind him and then took the gun from her. Margaret handed it over with a sense of shock. She would have fired it without hesitation if it had been necessary, and felt no qualms!

"How did you find out about the poison?" grunted Van Heerdon.

"She doesn't drink, so Craig had the lot and died right before us," provided Jan. "What a filthy method to use!"

"You must see I had to get rid of her. A woman always causes trouble when there are two men who want her. I can't let that sort of thing spoil my plans. I told them that."

"Stop talking and move," instructed Jan. "I shall shoot at the first false step you take —and it will be in a very painful place. Don't think you'll get a quick death from me. I want you alive and talking when we reach Myala, because you are going to clear Chris and me of any involvement in your activities."

"*Think*, man. You will be throwing away the biggest opportunity you will ever have in your life. Don't listen to *her*." He threw a contemptuous look at Margaret. "She told Craig you couldn't wait to get shot of her, but it's obvious you are besotted or you would never go back on an agreement in this suicidal manner. There are other women. Why be such a fool over one—and a born liar, at that?"

"Move!" repeated Jan. "You follow me, Maggie, and keep close or we may get separated." He gave Van Heerdon a push.

They went out into the night and started down the path. Even had Van Heerdon cried out it would have been lost in the raucous sounds which split the night. The drums, the stamping feet, and the off-key chanting continued as before with the addition of cries and shouts which echoed from first here, then there, as they made their way down towards the *kraal*. Margaret was not afraid. The whole thing had become so much beyond her normal experience it no longer seemed to be happening. The only thing she had to worry about was keeping that broad back in sight, for without Jan she would be lost.

They reached the outskirts of the *kraal* where the festivities had reached a frightening pitch. The dancers were in a complete frenzy. The movements they made had taken on a menacing flavour which was only one step from out and out aggression, and the beer was still flowing freely. All semblance of the dedicated rebels who fought for a cause had vanished beneath the call of an ancient civilization.

No wonder Mtubu had advised his white friends to stay in the cave that night!

The small procession skirted the clearing, keeping well out of sight, but Margaret's head thundered with the drumming of hands and feet. It seemed she could even *smell* pagan emotions in the smoke which rose from the circle of flaming torches, and mingled with the reek of cooking meat and sweating humanity. Suddenly she wanted to be free and back amongst her own people; she had seen enough of native Africa for the moment.

Jan led them round behind the camouflage nets which hung above the row of vehicles, and they halted while he did a rapid mental appraisal of the choice open to him. The larger trucks afforded more protection, but a jeep would be easier to manoeuvre along the narrow tracks he would have to follow. Stealing the thing would be easy enough—there was only a handful of men who could drive them so it would not occur to them to take precautions against theft—the problem would be getting out on to the track. Heavy netting covered with green and brown cloth pieces hung down three sides of this makeshift garage which meant the only way to drive out was straight across the compound where the dancing was taking place. The starting of the engine might go unnoticed in the general pandemonium, but without a couple of fifteen-foot props to hold up that net, all hopes of an unseen getaway were finished.

The keys were in the ignition of the first two jeeps, as he had expected, and he chose the second because the petrol tank registered FULL and because he had an easy route straight across the compound once he got going. The element of surprise was their best chance. He pushed Van Heerdon face downwards in the back and gave Margaret the revolver while he collected the keys from the entire row of vehicles and put them in his pocket.

"Jump in," he invited, taking the gun back. "We are going to leave here with a bang and I want you to keep right down until we are clear of the *kraal*. Are you ready?"

"Yes. Jan . . . I have complete faith in you to get us away."

"I wish I had," he murmured, completely missing the message she was trying to pass to him because of his concentration on matters in hand. "Get down and hold tight!"

The engine roared to life as headlamps blazed out across the writhing black bodies, and next minute, Margaret felt like a human pellet from a catapult as Jan adopted his Lotus technique to a military-jeep. As if that were not enough, two deafening cracks nearly split her eardrums as he fired into the air. The little she saw of the scene as the jeep swerved and skidded across the compound reminded her of riding the Ghost Train when she was a child. Black faces with staring eyes loomed and were gone, garish colours danced before her eyes, piercing shrieks mingled with the squealing of the tyres under duress, and a mad hotch-potch of smoke, flaming torches, leaves, white walls, and waving arms appeared out of the darkness and vanished as they changed direction yet again. It could only have taken a matter of seconds yet her eyes and ears missed nothing of the chaos they left behind them when the jeep rocked on to the track and went hell for leather along it. Neither did she miss a glimpse of that hated bird-mask which hid an evil man from the people who reverenced him. The vivid replica of a cruel beak and wicked eyes would haunt her dreams for some time to come.

"You can come up now." Jan's voice was reassuringly steady and sane. "I've kicked up merry hell at some parties in my time, but never like that. Are you all right?"

"Just about. How long will it take us to reach Myala? Does this track lead to the road which crosses the border?"

"No. I'm afraid we have to return to the *kraal* where we were taken prisoner and then find our way back to the access in the Reserve fence. To go over legitimately is impossible, for reasons which I should have thought were obvious."

"But you daren't return to that place," said Margaret. "Van Heerdon told us the men had all pledged to kill you if they saw you unshackled."

"I shall have to make sure they don't see me. It shouldn't be difficult. Most of them are probably at that celebration we have just ruined." He inclined his head to the back. "Is Van Heerdon still with us?"

Margaret glanced round. "All in a heap

in the corner. He doesn't look at all comfortable."

"Best news I've heard today!"

Margaret fell silent for a long while. Here she was, once more spending the hours of darkness by careering along in a stolen vehicle. Would she never occupy an African night in the erotic pleasure of having Jan prove to her that he knew of better ways to keep warm in bed?

By the time Jan slowed to a crawl and switched off his lights she was nearly asleep.

"We are getting near the *kraal*," he said in a low voice. "I'll go as far as I dare, then we'll have to abandon the jeep. "It's a long walk, Maggie."

"I know. I didn't enjoy the outward journey overmuch."

African dawns had the habit of surprising people, and now the headlamps were off, it was possible to distinguish the faint outline of the track, not by moonlight, as Margaret at first thought, but by the palest lifting of night. The jeep rolled silently along like a small boat being lifted on slight swell as tension tied knots in Margaret's stomach. Jan appeared calm and confident, and she sensed it was not simply a cover. His determination was born of cold, lucid thought, not the burning anger which had possessed him on the previous journey through here. Somewhere along the line, his restless spirit had come to terms with itself; the self-destructive quality of his nature had reached a compromise. He was never likely to tell her how it came about, for he kept all those things to himself, but one day she might perhaps receive a clue and put two and two together. For now, she was content to know that it had happened. He had told Van Heerdon: "You are going to clear Chris and me thereby establishing the fact that he had plans for his own future." She prayed he would be allowed one!

The jeep stopped on a bend. "This is the terminus," Jan said as he got out and pocketed the keys. "If we go any further we shall be within view of the *kraal*. Unfortunately, whoever happens to be still in residence will be up and about at dawn. Pity we couldn't have arrived an hour earlier!" He walked round to the back and hauled Van Heerdon out. "The same still applies," he warned him. "One sound and you'll be doubled up with pain."

The sandy-haired man looked pale in the grey light as he was pushed ahead through the scant undergrowth. Margaret followed closely behind as Jan explained that the going would be easier once they had skirted the *kraal* and joined the path they had used to come in by, but they had hardly gone thirty paces when movement to their left froze them in their tracks. The inhabitants of the *kraal* were indeed up and about!

Four tribesmen stood not far from the abandoned jeep, daring the fugitives to defy the power of their assegais. Margaret died inside as she thought all hope had gone, but Jan was thinking furiously. He had the gun, but it was useless against four weapons; his first shot might fell one man but it would bring certain death from the remaining three. There was one outside chance he could take, but if it didn't come off it would be the last thing he ever did. The men were slowly advancing so that it had to be now or never.

Margaret was trembling, the sweat standing out on her brow, as she waited for the black men to reach them, when her tattered nerves were shaken further. Jan fired two quick shots in succession, the first hit the jeep with a metallic thud, the second ricocheted off the metal side of the vehicle. Instantly, the jeep exploded into leaping orange flames as the spark caused by the ricochet ignited the petrol tank which had been pierced by the first bullet. It was a formidable sight! Where there had been a khaki vehicle, there was now a blazing furnace shooting fire and smoke into the lightening sky.

"Run!" yelled Jan, and she did, crashing through undergrowth which tore at her clothes and bare limbs, and leaping across obstacles like the nimblest of springboks, though how her legs supported her she would never know.

In the split second before flight, the photo-cells of her memory recorded the fact that the four ebony figures were transfixed with fear at this evidence of the flame-headed man's powers. Without the witch-doctor to induce super bravery, they were unwilling to challenge this terrible force. Gradually she became aware of heavy breathing beside her and realized Jan was hauling Van Heerdon along at great expense to his own energy.

"Leave him behind," she panted.

"Not on your life. He's my witness," returned Jan between grunts. "Bear right and we should reach the path."

The luminous light of full dawning day made the route instantly recognizable, and progress was a little easier for a while until the trees started getting denser and a pain in her side forced Margaret to stop.

"I can't, Jan," she gasped. "I can't run any more. Can we rest for a minute?"

"No chance. We must keep moving . . . but I'll slow the pace a bit, if I must." His chest was heaving and the strain of the last few days showed on his face in the harsh brilliance of what promised to be a glorious golden day. His large hand released its grip on Van Heerdon's arm. "You can go on ahead. Your pals at the *kraal* are not going to save you now you are in the hands of a fire-raiser. Get marching!"

That walk nearly finished Margaret. Her proud boast of being a strong, healthy girl seemed to prove a lie, but long walks in the bracing English countryside could hardly be compared with the trek through Africa following five days of the kind she had just spent. Jan amazed her. When he should be physically drained, the continued strength he summoned kept him going at a steady pace. A youth spent in the sunshine of this invigorating country, plus the fact that they came from a long line of sturdy farming stock, had given the Schroeder men constitutions which were not easily lowered . . . but she was not to know that!

Heat was beating down in waves upon their heads when the fence of Myala Game Reserve was reached. Jan found the gate easily, thanks to Margaret's not covering up evidence of it when she had come through two days before, and Van Heerdon was pushed into South Africa without ceremony before being followed by the man and girl. The thankfulness Margaret felt at being safely back in this country was completely ruined the next minute when Jan gave a loud exclamation.

"They've taken the bloody trucks!"

Sure enough, the jeep Craig had left behind and the stolen police truck were no longer parked beneath the trees, and all they could see was the shimmering, hazy landscape as it lay before them for mile after mile. There was a short return of the Jan she knew as he ranted and raved over the gross stupidity of whoever had removed the vehicles.

"If this is Chris's doing, I'll knock him flying when we meet. Surely his sense would tell him we had crossed the border this way and would therefore come back by the same route! God, how could he be so dense!"

"What do we do now?" asked Margaret when she could get a word in.

"Walk, that's what! Good thing you like fresh air—you are going to have any amount of it starting *now*."

"Jan, I'm not joking and I'm not playing sex games, as you call them, but I can't go on until I have had a rest. It seems I am not as tough as you thought. I'm sorry."

Something in her voice brought him to his senses and, for the first time, he really noticed the state she was in. Gone was that superior look he hated; the shining clean, wholesome girl who tempted but discouraged. Instead, there stood before him a tangle-haired, scruffy gypsy in torn clothes who seemed a lot smaller than he remembered, and who was fighting off tears of exhaustion. For some reason, he was reminded of himself as a boy tramping for miles behind his brothers and sisters until he was ready to drop.

"Yes . . . well, all right," he said. "Can you keep going until we get beyond those trees in the distance? I'd rather like to put some yards between us and this fence before we stop. I don't think we have been followed, but I'd rather not be sitting here if they should arrive on the other side."

"I think I can manage that," she agreed wearily, "and I'll try not to hold you up any longer than necessary."

During the short rest Margaret tried not to think of cool, clear water, but it was a hard struggle. Nobody spoke. Jan sat with his back to a tree, watching Van Heerdon through eyes slitted against the glare of the sun, trying desperately hard not to give in to sleep. It was one of the dangers of resting. Van Heerdon's face was white and shiny with sweat, but he would look even sicker when the prison gates closed behind him, thought Jan grimly.

They walked for two hours without a break until a sharp rise in the ground hid the way ahead from view.

"Okay. Five minutes' rest," said Jan, and Margaret slid thankfully to the ground. "Keep an eye on him while I climb to the top and see if there is a track anywhere near."

She nodded automatically and took the gun as Jan walked, still with a slight limp, up the bush-dotted slope to stand silhouetted against the sky. It was heavy and breathless beneath the trees, and the sounds of the *veld* disguised the faint humming, at first. As it grew louder, Jan's acute hearing identified it, making him tilt his head back with a surge of gladness.

"There's a plane," said Van Heerdon to Margaret. "It's Chris Schroeder."

"Where?" Her head went back and Van Heerdon's foot shot out to kick the revolver from her hand.

"JAN!" she screamed, but it was all over in a second. Van Heerdon had her arm twisted up behind her before Jan had had time to collect his wits.

"Don't move, or I swear I'll break her arm," he was warned.

The threat rooted Jan to the spot, but Van Heerdon knew that without the gun he had only the slenderest of advantages.

His kick had sent the weapon flying into the undergrowth, much further than he had bargained for, and the instinct for flight was too great to allow him the risk of stopping near Jan while he searched for it. But if he had lost the gun, then so had his adversary and no matter how determined Jan might be, he was hardly likely to risk the safety of the girl.

"How did you get free?" asked Jan tautly.

"You would have done better to make me comfortable in the cab of that jeep instead of throwing me in the back like so much merchandise. It didn't take me long to find a rough edge, and two hours or so are quite long enough to cut through thin cord. After that, it was a matter of waiting my chance. I knew I'd never have it all the time you had the gun, but she was fooled as easily as a babe."

Margaret looked upward through blurred eyes to the figure standing so still on the crest of the *kopjie*. "I'm sorry, Jan. I don't seem to be any good at fighting your battles, after all."

He had wanted to see her taken down a peg or two, make just one mistake to prove she was human! Right now, she was dirty, unattractive, and beaten to her knees with remorse, but it didn't give him any pleasure. The hot rage of possessive loyalty rushed through him as if she were one of his sisters . . . no, *more* than one of his sisters, and he took a quick step down the hill.

"Don't move!" screamed Van Heerdon wildly, and gave Margaret's arm a twist to add weight to his words.

Jan stopped and fought to control himself. He would have to *think* his way out of this one instead of rushing blindly at it as he usually did. His actions now were vitally important to the life and safety of the girl who had been through so much with him.

The helicopter appeared to be coming nearer so Van Heerdon moved, slowly backwards at first, until he and Margaret were hidden by foliage, then he grabbed her wrist and made her run. Soon, they were in thickening undergrowth searching for a hiding-place from the pursuers above and on the ground.

As she was pulled relentlessly on, Margaret had to step over knee-high bush which scratched her bare legs and tugged at her crumpled skirt. Her thick hair clung across her face, half-blinding her with dark strands, and her blouse stuck wetly to her back. Now and again, a grunt or rustle would indicate some other presence in that tangle of vegetation, but the creatures who scuttled from their path were ignorant and unheeding of the girl's predicament. The survival of the fittest was the lore of the bush, and it was each creature for himself, as they so well knew.

Her ankle turned on an uneven surface and she staggered, almost falling, but Van Heerdon turned to her and tugged at her wrist.

"Keep going," he grated out.

All manner of thoughts flicked though her mind during that nightmare scramble. Why had she not been more alert? Her proud boast that she could cope with any emergency was like rice paper beneath the onslaught of a hammer. All along, Jan had coped with the situation in a way which made her stupid attempts to take command look what they were—an interfering nuisance.

How he must hate her for her part in this

affair! What a ridiculous figure she must cut in his eyes! What had he called her . . . a militant do-gooder? All she had done was drag him down with her righteous attempts at guidance. She was the one who had needed guidance, not him. Why had she not realized from the beginning that her motive was not to convert him from his chosen path nor mother him in the manner of a small boy? From that day at Sea Point, the emotion driving her to remain beside him had been love . . . a misplaced conception of it, perhaps, but love, nevertheless. It was heartbreaking that she should cause his ultimate downfall.

In this blanket of misery she stumbled after Van Heerdon, stopping when he stopped, and moving on when a jerk on her arm told her to. The vegetation was thicker here and the man was pushing a way through head-high growth, sweating profusely and growing more and more savage. Suddenly, he broke through into a clearing and stopped dead. There, in the centre, lay an ancient Cape Buffalo who had chosen this place as somewhere quiet to rest from the heat of the day. He was old, he was tired, and he was infuriated by this intruder.

Van Heerdon froze at the sight of the great horned animal, but not so the buffalo at the blurred shape of its irritant. The beast lumbered to its feet and lowered the great head with an outraged bellow.

"No!" screamed Van Heerdon, and turned, but Margaret was in his way, so he ran forward across the clearing in a mad panic to gain the safety of the trees. The buffalo's horns caught the man's legs below the knees and sent him sprawling on the dry grass. It took a matter of seconds for the angry animal to turn, and the same time for Van Heerdon to be trampled and gored beyond recognition. The grunts of the incensed beast and the screams of his victim rang in Margaret's ears, and as she watched, it seemed as though the tribal drums were beating again, louder ever louder, until her whole body was shaking with them.

Tiring of an adversary who had no fight left in him, the buffalo became conscious that his peace was still threatened. His weak eyes registered another blur by the trees, but his superb sense of smell told him he had not removed the menace entirely and he swung his head round towards Margaret. The rhythm of the drums had quickened, and heat seemed to be pushing her down into the earth. Her face was wet and her vision blurred as the creature charged across the clearing, but a total immobility had descended on the girl's limbs, rooting her to the spot.

The impact came sooner than she expected, and from a different direction. Something hit her from the side knocking her into the scrub where her back was badly grazed on thick thorn branches, and her head made contact with a tree trunk in a deafening crack. Almost at once, a similar crack followed by the sound of a heavy weight falling into vegetation! The paralysing grip on her brain suddenly lifted as she realized the cracks had been gun shots, and the buffalo was lying lifeless a mere ten yards from where she lay. The vivid sky above the circle of tree-tops was suddenly full of wheeling birds and the quick moment of silence was broken again by harsh squawks. Next minute, Jan was there, kneeling beside her with that same look blazing in his eyes that he had had when he drove the police truck to Myala.

"Did you kill it?" she asked weakly.

"Yes. Sorry if I spoiled your opportunity to study the Cape Buffalo in its natural habitat."

She flung herself at him to be enclosed in his arms and was still there ten minutes later when a party of Rangers and policemen broke into the clearing from the opposite side.

The return to headquarters in a helicopter was extremely swift. In no time at all she was lying in the bed she had occupied before, having been given a bromide by the police doctor, who had also tended her many cuts. They had both been given a meal, but Jan was facing a barrage of questions which were not exactly friendly enquiries.

The voices of the men on the veranda carried on the still air, and she was kept awake by the growing fear that Jan was gradually being talked down. She heard him tell the police the whole story, ending with how he had seen the revolver from his elevated position on the hill where the sun glinting on the metal had given him the advantage over the man on level ground. He had followed Van Heerdon's progress through the thornbrush which had been made easy by the fact that the other man was a city dweller and had no experience of stealthy movement in the wilds. The noise of the hideous death beneath the hoofs of the buffalo had guided him to the spot in time to save Margaret, and the gunshots had indicated their presence to the touring police parties.

She then heard Chris's voice, so like his brother's, tell how he had arrived two days ago, as arranged, to find a serious state of affairs. Craig Barker had vanished *without* reporting Russell Martin's death to the authorities, and Jan and Margaret had taken off after him despite the beating the Rangers reported Jan had been given. Chris had instructed one of the Rangers to contact the Game Reserve governors, and took off to fly over the Reserve to look for vehicles. The jeep and police truck were discovered empty, and when Chris gave the police the number of the vehicle, they traced it to Alwynsrus. An immediate visit to the station there proved very lucky because the man who had been sent by Van

Heerdon to "deal" with Sergeant De Wet was caught very nicely in the same net as the iniquitous police officer.

As soon as the arms were discovered the police tightened up their security and set a detailed investigation in motion. The outcome of it was that Chris had been under police surveillance while the search went on for Jan and Craig Barker. It didn't take long for the police to decide the two men had crossed the border and a constant watch was kept on that area of the Reserve while the police on the other side were alerted. The girl's part in it was unknown, but the opinion was that she must be an innocent participant who was being used in some way.

The last thing she heard before drifting off to sleep was Jan listing all the details of Van Heerdon's contacts for the hoped-for international arms traffic, and the police Captain telling him he was also under surveillance, pending a full enquiry into Schroeder Freight Limited.

"I'm sorry about this, Chris," he said in his familiar deep voice. "Van Heerdon could have cleared you of any blame."

"We've nothing to worry about," came

the answer. "You may have been a bit wild, at times, but I know you could never get involved in anything like this. You're too loyal!"

"He's late!" grumbled Chris, looking at his watch for the fifth time. "You'd think he'd make an effort on Christmas day."

"He has," said Margaret from the window. "Listen!"

The orange Lotus roared to a halt outside the house at Sea Point, and Jan burst in with his usual gusto.

"Hallo, Helen . . . Maggie . . ." he smiled at the two women then; "Chris, I've been doing some calculations and I reckon I can save that Dakota, after all. Look, here are the preliminary figures I made." He took a slip of paper from his pocket, then stopped short at Chris's expression. "What's up?"

"Merry Christmas," said his brother pointedly.

The eagerness left Jan's face. "Oh lord! After that phone call from Brigadier Boetman I started planning where we would go from here, and completely forgot about anything else."

"What phone call?" asked Helen calmly.

"Hasn't he contacted you yet? He will! They think they have enough evidence to clear us on the gun-running charge. The police over there have smoked-out most of the rebels and linked the organization with the packing firm here in Cape Town, as well as other small fry in this area. According to evidence given in statements by various witnesses, Brigadier Boetman is inclined to believe my story, so it looks as if you are free of any charge, Chris."

"What about you?" asked Margaret.

He turned to her and raised his eyebrows. "I am guilty of accepting cargo I haven't personally checked, breaking out from arrest, locking two policemen in their own cell, and making off with a police vehicle while rendering the other one immobile. Sounds awful, put like that, but he hinted that, in view of the outcome of all these actions, he is prepared to turn a blind eye, providing I promise to keep out of any further schemes which propose making money faster than advisable."

"I should think so," she said. "Not only did you expose the gun-running, you enabled them to discover the unsavoury Sergeant De Wet."

His face lit in a smile. "The case against *him* will go on for days, I hear. They intend throwing the book at him in a big way, and when he has served his sentence, he'll be damned lucky to get employment anywhere —that's if he is not past retiring age by then. They'll pull him apart in court so he'll never again be given a position of trust."

"And the witch-doctor?" asked Margaret.

He shook his head. "Not a chance! Although it's obvious he and his lads passed the arms on to Mtubu, and were indirectly concerned with the guerrilla movement, they can't get witnesses or positive evidence to prove it. He's a crafty man—they all are or they'd never hold such sway over the people. However, he is going to be closely watched from now on, though I doubt if he will ever be caught at anything they can arrest him for."

"That awful bird-mask still haunts me," she said. "I hated him for what he did to you."

"Yes," put in Chris. "I was telling Margaret only this morning about the time *we* left you with a noose around your neck. Do you remember?"

There was only the barest hesitation before Jan said carefully, "Very well. You have no idea how bloody stupid I felt when you turned up that evening."

Chris gave a rueful grin. "How do you think *I* felt being thrashed in your presence as if I were a kid of your own age! It took me weeks to recover from that humiliation."

"It took me slightly longer."

"Let's not dwell on things like that," said Helen, seeing the look on Margaret's face. "The twins will be dashing in at any moment to see if you really have brought those model aircraft you promised them, Jan."

"Have I ever broken a promise to them?" he asked with a hurt expression which fooled her not a bit. "You cut me to the quick with your doubts of my truthfulness."

She laughed, hardly able to believe the subtle change in him these last few days. "You are every inch a Schroeder! You can charm your way out of anything."

"You can say that again," put in Margaret feelingly.

He turned to her. "I have a present for you, too."

"What is it . . . a one-way ticket to England?"

He ignored that and took an envelope from his pocket. "A letter from Doctor Marais, who is taking over as Warden of Myala. I met him once when I was staying at the Reserve, so I telephoned to check that he wishes to continue our contract to fly supplies in each month. While I was speaking to him I mentioned your problem regarding studying. This is an invitation to Myala so that he can discuss the possibility of your working there." A quick grin. "He is over fifty and has a wife there with him. I told him we'd fly up in the New Year, but there are a few things I'd like to get straight before we do. If anything goes wrong on *this* trip I won't stand any meddling. By trailing after me you landed yourself in a situation no woman should be in. Have you any idea how I felt when I saw that buffalo charge you?" He shook his head. "No. From now on you do as you are told in emergencies. Is that clear?"

"Perfectly," she replied, trying to control the feeling of bubbling exaltation which threatened to send her rushing at him. "Does that also apply to on-the-spot medical treatment?"

The brown of his eyes deepened as they took in the smile playing round her mouth, and he remembered her courage and determination.

"Just get in a little more practice with a needle before you try any more of those cattle injections," he said roughly, "and a little feminine sympathy would do wonders for a patient's morale."

"If you propose flying Margaret to Myala again you'll take a decent aircraft this time," said Chris. "One which won't get struck by lightning."

The two women waited for an angry outburst which didn't come.

"All right, all right," said Jan equably. "I know I'll never live that down . . . but I'll save the Dakota yet!"

"Forget it. You'll need all the money you have to recover from the purchase of that monster parked outside. Besides, the Board of Directors has decided that, if we have to have another aircraft, we'll have a more

330

modern one—if only to avoid a repetition of this affair. You are to be given a cheque for twenty-five thousand rands, and instructions to get the best you can. I think the rest of the family realizes it is time we expanded slightly, and you are the expert when it comes to the mechanical side."

Margaret watched the two men eagerly discussing their future plans, but her eyes lingered on the freckled face she had come to know so well, and saw her future written there. It was impossible to catch this lion by the mane; when he was ready, he would willingly approach anyone who had earned his trust and respect. She had that now . . . and something more. A show of aggression, the instinct to protect his partner and the desire for female attentions were courtship traits in the male of the species, and Jan had just displayed them all! He might not be ready to admit it, but a little gentle encouragement from her would help . . . and she was flying to Myala with him next week!